Princess Ben

Princess Ben

Being a Wholly Truthful Account of Her Various Discoveries and Misadventures, Recounted to the Best of Her Recollection, in Four Parts

WRITTEN BY

CATHERINE GILBERT MURDOCK

Houghton Mifflin Company
Boston 2008

www.houghtonmifflinbooks.com

The text of this book is set in Perpetua.

Library of Congress Cataloging-in-Publication Data

Murdock, Catherine Gilbert.

Princess Ben : being a wholly truthful account of her various discoveries and misadventures, recounted to the best of her recollection, in four parts / written by Catherine Gilbert Murdock.

p. cm.

Summary: A girl is transformed, through instruction in life at court, determination, and magic, from sullen, pudgy, graceless Ben into Crown Princess Benevolence, a fit ruler of the kindgom of Montagne as it faces war with neighboring Drachensbett.

ISBN 978-0-618-95971-6

[1. Fairy tales. 2. Princesses—Fiction. 3. Kings, queens, rulers, etc.—Fiction. 4. Magic—Fiction. 5. Courts and courtiers—Fiction. 6. Self-actualization (Psychology)—Fiction.] I. Title.

PZ8.M942Pri 2008

[Fic]—dc22

2007034300

Manufactured in the United States of America

QUM 10 9 8 7 6 5 4 3 2 1

To James,

my prince and super genius

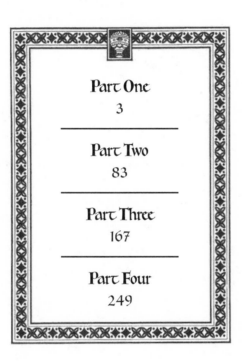

Part One
3

Part Two
83

Part Three
167

Part Four
249

Having for many decades been forced to endure ever more ridiculous tales of the circumstances surrounding my coming of age, holding my tongue through each long-winded narrative for fear that my cautious interjections would only prolong the blather, I now in the solitude of my dotage at last permit myself the indulgence of correcting the erroneous legends and embroidered falsehoods that to this day expand, heady as yeast, across the land. The country people say that to understand a sausage one must know the pig; so it is that this white-haired sow (as I dub myself with great fondness) is uniquely suited to provide the most accurate chronology. I freely acknowledge that had I myself not experienced every moment recorded herein, my narration at times would sound worse than implausible, but nonetheless, accept my solemn oath that each anecdote and interaction chronicled within these pages is as truthful and exact as my recollections permit.

Part One

In which fate deals me a savage blow,

leaving me to my own pitiably meager devices

ONE

How many times I have wondered what my fate might have been had I accompanied my parents that rainy spring morning. Such musings, I recognize, are more than a trifle insane, for envisioning what *might have been* has no more connection to our own true reality than a lunatic has to a lemon. Nevertheless, particularly in those bleak moments that at times overwhelm even the happiest of souls, my thoughts return to my dear mother and father, and again I marvel at the utter unpredictability of life, and the truth that our futures are so often determined not by some grand design or deliberate strategy but by an ordinary run-of-the-mill head cold.

To be honest, my sickness did not occur completely by chance. I had exhausted myself in preparing for my fifteenth birthday fete the week before, had gorged myself during the party on far too many sweets, and had then caught a chill during a lengthy game of stags and hunters with my guests in the twilight forest. Now, however, denying all my symptoms, I begged to join my parents.

"I have to go!" I insisted from my sick bed. "It's my *grandfather.*"

My mother sighed. "Your grandfather would never approve of his granddaughter of all people making herself twice as ill on his account." She replaced the cloth, soaked in her own herbal concoction, on my forehead, and coaxed some tea across my lips. "Why don't you draw him a picture instead? I promise to leave it in a place of honor."

"A *picture?*" I scoffed. "I wish you'd realize I'm not a *child.*"

She kissed my flushed cheeks with a smile. "Try to sleep, darling. We'll be back before dusk."

These words, too, I ponder. No matter how loudly I may have denied it, all evidence demonstrated I was still very much a child. After all, I had brought this illness upon myself. Worse, I had sensed the head cold brewing yet petulantly refused to follow my mother's advice, so sacrificing that pinch of prevention for cup after cup of homemade cure. My bedroom remained crowded with piles of fairy tales, many of the pages illuminated with my own crude drawings, and dolls in varied displays of dishabille. How easy it would have been for my mother—indeed, were the tables turned, I would have so responded without hesitation—to point out my childishness. *I told you so* may be painless to utter, but that does not diminish the anguish these four words inflict upon a listener already in pain. That my mother held her tongue and gave me only love when I merited chiding demonstrates her empathy. So many times in the decades since I have reminded myself of her innate compassion, and on my best days have striven to match it.

At the time, though, I simply sulked, and so my father found me as he strode in to wish me well. Even in the gloom of that overcast morning he looked magnificent, his dress armor polished to a high gleam and his prince's circlet, excavated from the woolen trunks for its semiannual outing, shining against his graying curls.

He settled on my bedside with a clank or two. "'Tis a great shame you can't join us today."

I pouted. "I could go. If you let me."

"And have your mother put my head on a stake? Do you have any notion what that would do to my handsome good looks?"

I refused to be cheered.

He eyed me with a twinkle. "What if I returned with a dragon?"

Through enormous focus, I maintained my glower.

"A wee green one that whistled like a kettle? It could roast chestnuts for you on winter mornings."

Despite my best efforts, up crept the corners of my mouth. "And warm your chilblains when you're old," I added.

"'Ben,' I'd call out, 'where's that blasted dragon of yours? My old toes are freezing!'"

"And I'll go and find the dragon—"

"Where it's playing with my grandchildren—"

"And ask it, quite nicely, to come inside and attend to the needs of His Royal Highness, the Prince of Montagne." I giggled; I could not help it.

"Oh, bosh! You say *that* to a dragon and it'll gobble me up, as sure as salt's salt."

"And what would that do to your handsome good looks?" I teased him.

"Improve them, I'd wager," he answered with a grin. "Now, you be good and drink that wretched concoction, and I'll take you up there next week. Just the two of us."

"Truly? With a picnic? A big one?"

"Absolutely." He, too, kissed my cheeks, and with a last exaggerated bow in my direction, he clattered down the stairs.

Wrapping myself in a quilt, I crept to the window. In the courtyard below, Mother frowned as she struggled to fit her own golden princess circlet, for she had little skill at ceremony. With a flourish of trumpets, Uncle Ferdinand appeared at the great entrance to the castle proper, looking every inch the king in his robes of state. Unlike my father, Uncle Ferdinand truly was handsome, tall and lean and solemn. At his side stepped the group's martial escort, Xavier the Elder, a grizzled warrior who had shaved so thoroughly that several nicks still oozed blood. Queen Sophia appeared as well, displaying the precise gestures and expressions expected of a woman of her rank.

A quintet of soldiers played a military hymn, and then Mother, Father, Ferdinand, and Xavier strode across the drawbridge through a double phalanx of saluting guards. Father glanced back to smile a last greeting at me as Mother slipped her arm through his and lay her head on his shoulder. His armor must have been cold, given the unseasonable chill of the day, but the love between them transcended such trivial discomfort.

Seeing them off, the queen stood at attention for exactly

the amount of time that a queen should, and then with a cool flick of her gown turned back toward the castle, the footmen falling in behind her.

Alone at last, the quilt about my shoulders, I sighed as I considered all the tasks that awaited me. A wool vest I had begun for Father the previous autumn lay half finished, my efforts immobilized by a plethora of dropped stitches. Clearly it would not serve him this winter; at the rate I was progressing, years could pass before the thing warmed him. My mother had delegated to me the task of transcribing her grandmother's yellowed recipes, the goal being to learn the art of cooking while improving my penmanship. Unfortunately the assignment always left me famished, rooting through the kitchen pantries like an autumn bear. Hunger was a burden I could not tolerate for even a heartbeat, a truth that my physique amply demonstrated. Simply glancing at the stack of stained and curling recipes sent my stomach to growling.

Outside, the master of hounds returned with his pack, the dogs gleeful and wet from a long run and a swim in the Great River. But even their prancing enthusiasm did not lift my own misery. With only the ubiquitous murmur from the soldiers' barracks to comfort me, I crept back into bed, seeking refuge from the oppressive mist that cloaked the castle's turrets. Perusing my shelves, I could not find one volume to satisfy me. The fairy tales I had read countless times. The more recent additions held even less interest: dry histories of Montagne, geometry textbooks, a medical treatise on bloodletting that my mother appeared never to have opened and that she now put to use as a bookend.

I squirmed further under the covers. My mind drifted, wondering if the foursome had yet arrived at my grandfather's tomb, what they would say there in his honor. I had practiced my own speech for weeks, and had been quite proud of my little poem praising the Badger's courage, the last stanza in particular:

You perished to save all of us.
I hope your armor never rusts.

A dramatic conclusion, I believed at the time, though it now occurred to me that any armor entombed with a corpse for thirty-odd years would doubtless experience some corrosion. This realization only deepened my malaise.

At last I drifted into a fitful sleep. Though slumber should remove us from the trials of our waking life—surely I always settled my head with this expectation, and ere this day had always found satisfaction—my present nap did rather the opposite. Almost at once, it seemed, my rest was disturbed by haunting images of the castle corridors. Not my familiar apartment, constructed scarce a century earlier with the new perimeter fortifications, but the castle proper, noble and ancient, with walls as thick as three men, and the Montagne hedgehog, emblem of the kingdom, carved in countless obscure corners.

In this dream as I walked the corridors, one of these hedgehogs uncurled itself and turned to stare at me with black, unblinking eyes. Try as I might, I could not escape this piercing glare; I was trapped as utterly as a fish on a hook, though unlike a fish I could not even thrash about, for the paralysis of nightmare held me immobilized. Larger and larger those eyes grew, until their impenetrable blackness filled my vision. I had the sensation, provided by that sporadic omniscience that accompanies dream-state, that I must creep forward, though I had not a notion in the world whereto I was headed, or whether the floor below me would dissolve in abyss. At once a voice, opaque and unidentifiable, filled my ears: "It is time."

With a great jerk, I awoke to darkness, perspiration drenching my body. My fever, at least, had broken. Gradually my beating heart slowed; I was in my own bed, my parents nearby, with naught to fear. The flickering shadows came only from the parade ground lanterns that I had known every night of my life.

Another consideration troubled my mind. My parents had promised to return by dusk, and clearly night had fallen. They should not have left me to sleep, I thought crossly, particularly given that awful dream. Did they not notice my tossing and turning?

I wandered into the kitchen, chiding words on my lips.

But the kitchen stood empty, the hearth cold. My irritation progressed to unease, highlighted by the torch-lit shadows that moved ever more rapidly across the walls, casting Mother's jarred remedies and bundled herbs into grotesque shapes. I shivered.

The drum of hoofbeats across the drawbridge caught my attention. Faint though the noise be, as soldier's daughter I had been trained from early age to note such sounds as might bode ill. I hurried to the window. Outside, a rider on a steaming horse gestured to guards already racing to quarters. Other horsemen hurried in, and townsfolk as well, as torches smoked between the raindrops.

Anxiously I threw a cape over my nightgown and made

my way outside. "Ancienne herself is crying," a woman muttered as she huddled beneath a dripping eave. A trio of soldiers on horseback, desperate to pass, shouted at the growing throng.

Suddenly a great cry arose in Market Town, followed by a thick silence, as if a hand descending from the heavens snuffed the living noise from the earth. The crowd parted to reveal a soldier leading a horse and wagon. In the sputtering light I could not make out the soldier's face, but the slump of his shoulders announced tragedy. The shaggy draft horse moved with the inherent nobility of all honest laborers, and so caught up was I in the power of this image that it took me a moment to realize the wagon, still loaded with some poor farmer's seed potatoes, contained a body as well. Only when the women beside me dropped to their knees did I notice the golden crown and realize I was beholding the bloody, rain-drenched corpse of my uncle, King Ferdinand.

Behind the cart came other soldiers, and a spontaneous procession of mourning citizens, the women, and many men, weeping openly. Silence grew as the throng drained into the castle's inner courtyard; then the drawbridge rang again with clopping hoofbeats. Another cart horse appeared, led by a pair of heartbroken soldiers.

Shaking, willing myself to awaken from this horrible nightmare, I clung to the wall behind me. The cart passed. Inside I beheld the waxen and immobile face of my mother.

I staggered forward, deaf to my own cries, and clambered beside her. I twined my fingers in her icy hand, wiping the sodden hair and bits of grass from her face, searching for her sweet smile. Her body, still and twisted, did not move but for the rocking of the cart.

I spread my cape over us both, doing my best to protect her from the rain. "You'll be fine," I murmured. "Just fine. Sleep now . . ." Though my mind knew she had left this world, my heart could not accept it, and I poured all the love I knew onto her lifeless form. Suddenly, I turned to the soldiers: "Father! Where is my father?"

They shifted, avoiding my eye.

"Please! Tell me, I beg you . . ."

At last, one of them spoke. "No one knows, miss." He swallowed convulsively. "He's gone."

* * * *

All that night King Ferdinand's body lay outside the castle. Every Montagne man, woman, and child capable of travel came to pay respects, their tears mingling with the desolate rain, and by morning the windows, flagpoles, and people were draped in black crepe as the wool merchants of Market Town emptied their warehouses.

My mother lay in the castle courtyard as well, and I refused to leave her side. I can scarce recall any detail from that swirl of sodden pain, the useless words of solace offered by neighbors and friends. I craved every moment with her, and moreover wanted to hear immediately any news whatsoever of my father. Hour by hour, soldiers replaced the lantern at her head with a fresh taper. Search parties, filthy and exhausted, returned for reinforcements, and by their stance alone I could tell they had naught to report. The entire valley roiled with confusion, the terror abetted by the downpour. Dawn arrived at last, lightening the cold fog, with no sign of Xavier the Elder or my father. Soldiers returning from the tomb reported in whispers that their nocturnal efforts had reduced the site to mud, defeating any further tracking. The news drove me closer still to my mother's icy corpse.

As tradition dictated, interment took place that afternoon. A formal memorial service would occur months or years hence following completion of a tomb for King Ferdinand, and for my mother as well, a princess by marriage if not temperament. At the moment, however, the bodies required burial without delay, however much the sky cried its relentless drizzle.

In the confusion and turmoil, I was overlooked or indulged by everyone, allowed to accompany my mother's body to the gravesite and to give her one last embrace as she was sealed in a simple wooden coffin. I still wore the heavy cape I had donned when first I left our home so many hours before, and the sopping wool dripped cold water down my neck whenever I peered toward Ancienne, forever anticipating that the fog would part to reveal some sign of my father. The chill mingled with my grief and exhaustion, and standing at the graveside, listening to the drone of the priest, his words devoid of intimacy or comfort, I broke down completely.

"Why do you all stand here?" I shrieked, my voice carrying across the throng. "Why aren't you looking for him? He's out there, somewhere, and you don't even care! I'll find him myself, then. I will! I'll find him myself . . ." My rush toward the mountain was stopped at once by kind hands, and unkind hands as well, accompanied by hisses that I must behave myself before the queen, who stood at the graves' head in a black veil, as rigid and unmoving as a corpse.

Collapsing into sobs, I did not notice the crowd stiffen,

the whispers as mourners craned to observe some late arrivals to the cemetery. Not until I was led away did the sight register: a score of horsemen clothed in black, their scabbards empty and pikes dulled, incongruous in some discordant way. Only when I was returned to our empty apartment, still sobbing, did I realize in an ill-timed flash of clarity that each of the horsemen wore on his chest the scarlet dragon of Drachensbett.

For my grandfather's killers—our country's sworn enemies—to appear at this moment, and late for the ceremony at that . . . My father, I knew, would want to hear this most disturbing news. I must tell him. He must return so that I could.

TWO

The country of Montagne consists of a single rich valley contained on three sides by snow-topped mountains. The fourth side, conversely, drops precipitously into a cliff accessible only by switchbacks long ago carved into its flank. Swift streams lace the valley floor, weaving into the Great River, which plunges over this cliff in a most wondrous, ever-changing waterfall. Strategically placed aside this cascade at the valley's sole point of entry is the ancient stronghold of Chateau de Montagne. Its massive stone walls rise sheer from the cliff itself, while its valley side protects the bustling community of Market Town quite as a mother hen nurtures her chicks.

Looming over valley, castle, and town is Montagne, the kingdom's namesake, its symbol, and in many respects its soul, so well demonstrated by the word *montagne* itself. Not "the mountain" or "the grand mountain" or "our mountain," but simply "mountain," as though no other hill or alp or Everest had any conceivable significance. Indeed, since time past knowing valley people have spoken of this cloud-banked pinnacle as a living creature with powers beyond human intelligence. "Ancienne," they call her. Old One. "She's brooding today, Ancienne is," men will say, watching storm clouds gather around the peak. Soon enough, a brutal wind will sweep down Montagne's slopes, sending shepherds hurrying to their flocks, and housewives to their laying hens.

According to Montagne legend, the mountain has forever been the abode of giants. Long ago a traveling pair of sorcerers, husband and wife, scaled the cliff into the valley, and the woman cured the giants' chilblains with ointments and the gift of fire. In gratitude, the giants built Chateau de Montagne out of the living rock of Ancienne, and from that castle the couple founded the kingdom of Montagne, using their magic to shield the country and its people from harm.

As a child I adored hearing this legend and insisted my father recite it almost nightly. It is perhaps significant that the two of us combined this story with that of Drachensbett, our neighbor and eternal foe. That kingdom possessed the land surrounding Montagne, which they called *Drachensbett,* or "Dragons' Bed." They asserted that dragons occupied Ancienne's icy peak and that their royal family itself originated from these mythic beasts.

Our country had no objection to such tales, for every people has a right to its foundation myths. But unlike Montagne, Drachensbett could not keep its spoons out of other men's soups. In its rapacious lust for expansion, it had attacked our small kingdom countless times throughout our history. Were it not for the natural protection of the cliff, the strategic placement of Chateau de Montagne, and our own innate determination, Montagne would be but a shire ruled by the self-proclaimed descendants of dragons.

To be sure, independence required no small amount of vigilance. Threat of war a century earlier had spurred expansion of the perimeter walls; within these new walls were built fresh barracks and the apartment above that served as my childhood home. In my grandfather's time, Drachensbett again assembled an army. My grandfather, King Henri—"the Badger," as he was dubbed for his relentlessness (and also, I have been told, for his short yet burly physique)—employed every possible diplomacy against this more powerful opponent, at the same time improving his military defenses until the castle could not have more perfectly resembled its spiky hedgehog emblem. Unlike hedgehogs, however, men are susceptible to the promise of gold. Drachensbett agents enticed a malleable Montagne guard to open the gates of Market Town one dark night. Too late alerted, Henri nevertheless gathered his men, and, true to his name, led a ferocious counterattack against the menace. So fiercely did the Badger fight that the Drachensbett men were forced back across the drawbridge, through Market Town, and down the cliff. What had begun as assured conquest culminated in a rout. Not without price, however, for the Badger's glorious efforts left him mortally wounded, and he perished ere the sun rose over the unconquered lands of Montagne.

My Uncle Ferdinand, though scarce in his majority, accepted the crown and scepter that very morn, and rallied his disheartened people. His first act as king was to commission a tomb for his father high on the slopes of Ancienne. Each May on the anniversary of this famous battle, Ferdinand and his brother Walter, my father, traveled to the tomb to honor their father's passing. My mother and I joined them, as did the most honored veterans who had fought at the Badger's side.

On these outings, enthralled as I was with tales of Ancienne's magical occupants, I searched for elves and giants' footprints but found only chiding songbirds, and once glimpsed a fox disappearing into the brush. While the adults spoke and prayed, I tied chains of wildflowers that I laid across my grandfather's tomb in a manner my parents, to my pride, seemed to find quite moving. The solemnity of the holiday and the beauty of the mountainside bedecked in flowers and emerald grass, the cloud-shrouded pinnacle splitting the heavens far above my head, always left a lasting impression.

❀ ❀ ❀ ❀

Curiously, for all the suffering and fear that Drachensbett has inflicted on my country and my family, I have very few childhood memories of our foe. Just as a violent sea storm fades in exhaustion, leaving the coastline to heal itself, so too did Drachensbett's martial impulse wane—so it appeared—in the three decades following the Badger's victory, and both countries flourished in the relief of peace.

I do recall one exchange following my father's return from yet another diplomatic expedition to clarify our nations' precise boundaries, for the snowbound heights of Ancienne, impassable as they were, had never been mapped, and this predicament sporadically occupied the governments' attention.

"Renaldo"—the current king of Drachensbett—"has a

son, you know," he informed me as I made short work of the sweets he had brought, a Drachensbett specialty of dried fruit, caramel, and nuts.

"Yes," my mother said. "A most difficult labor, I heard . . ." As a healer, she was forever seasoning our conversation with medical gossip.

He grinned. "Well, the boy's healthy enough now. Perhaps you two will marry someday."

I interrupted my gorging long enough to pantomime violent retching.

"Walter!" Mother scolded. She blamed him, with good cause, for my unruly behavior.

I struggled to speak through the gluey caramel: "Did you—did you see any dragons?"

"Oh, all kinds." He grinned. "A fire-breathing kind, another green one that—"

"They have nothing of the sort!" my mother informed me. "At least not when they're awake."

"Come now, Pence," my father began, addressing her by her childhood nickname, derived from the fact she was small as a penny. "It's naught to get riled about—"

"What do you mean, 'awake'?" I asked.

"She means they only dream about dragons."

"You mean there aren't *really* dragons? Not even on Ancienne?" Disappointment surged through me.

Mother smiled. "I'm afraid not, darling. And the sooner they stop blathering about dragons' beds and dragon blood, the better off we'll all of us be. Now go wash your hands before you begin attracting flies."

I could not help but wonder, that night and later, why my father would even mention my marrying someone who came from a country that my mother so obviously disliked. I recall wondering that distinctly, while somehow missing the obvious connection that this boy was a prince and that I, the niece of a king, was a princess.

❀ ❀ ❀ ❀

So often warfare is preceded by rumors that swirl about the populace, triggering anxious preparations. But the murder of King Ferdinand struck the peaceful residents of Montagne without the slightest murmur of forewarning.

The royal party, as best could be understood, had been ambushed as they stood at the Badger's tomb. My mother had been attacked first, stabbed in the back a half-dozen times. Ferdinand must have raced to her aid, for his forearms, shoulders, and face had been slashed repeatedly, by a poisoned blade no less. Naught but poison could explain his perishing, for his wounds were not fatal, and his skin even in death bore an unnatural greenish tint.

As for my father and Xavier the Elder, no sign could be found of them whatsoever. The first search party, sent out by the queen when the foursome failed to return at the designated hour, scoured the tomb site, navigating more like ships than men through the rain. A second party, led by Xavier the Younger (son of Xavier the Elder and second in command of the Montagne army after my father), had climbed higher and farther, to no avail. For all their crawling and calling, no footprint or blaze or drop of blood could be found in the mire. By all appearances, the two men had vanished.

I knew little of this that first hellish night as I shivered beside my mother's corpse. My mind when it functioned at all dwelt on my own grief and loss, not the details of her injuries or the identity of her vicious killers. Even in my dull pain, however, listening to soldiers prepare the castle for attack, I recognized the murders as an act of war. To name the precise moment when my suspicions fixed upon Drachensbett would be impossible; rather, it came upon me subconsciously, as a subtle noise invades one's dreams until, without realization, one is awake. Drachensbett had an established history of subterfuge. How great a difference between bribery and assassination, particularly when the ultimate goal is the same? That country knew the anniversary of the Badger's death, having caused it, and knew as well of the traditional visit to his tomb. The murder of King Ferdinand would throw Montagne into disarray; the disappearance of Prince Walter, head of Montagne's army, would double this confusion. Whether my father was kidnapped or murdered I knew not. In optimistic moments, I fancied he had escaped their clutches and was even now guarding or being guarded by Xavier the Elder, preparing their return. At these times I despised Drachensbett more than ever for sowing my confusion with seeds of hope that slowly withered as no word came.

❖ ❖ ❖ ❖

This chronicle explains, I pray, my dumbfounded shock over the appearance of a troupe of Drachensbett soldiers at the interment. Judging from the reaction of the folk crowding those two fresh graves, I had not been alone in my suspicions. Whether the foreigners did not perceive the mutters and glares aimed in their direction or chose to ignore them I could not deduce, and I longed even more for my father, who, I knew, would be able to explain this inexplicable act.

I had been bundled away from the burial service by Frau Lungonaso, a townswoman who often worked for us as housekeeper. The woman had made little effort over the years to withhold her disapproval of my rearing, and I am sure she viewed the present tragedy as retribution for my parents' indulgence of their daughter. Back in our apartment, she stripped me of my sodden garments, muttering under her breath about pneumonia.

Little did I note the woman's complaints. Nigh catatonic with grief, exhaustion, and chill, I offered no resistance to her rough handling, and even consented to a bath, where I sat immune to the warmth. My heartache suppressed even my head cold, it seemed, for my earlier discomfort registered not in the slightest. Outside, the ominous sky pressed down; the hushed voices and quiet steps added to the unease. Dimly I registered a knock at the front door and a hurried conversation.

At once Frau Lungonaso bustled in without consideration of my modesty. "Hurry up now," she snapped. "Quick—it's important."

My heart leapt in its cage. "My father! He has been found?"

"What? No! The queen wishes an audience. Come, come, out of there at once!"

What followed would have the makings of an absurd comedy were it not so horribly real. My best dress—for one only meets the queen in her best even if the queen be one's aunt—was soiled with jam on both front and back, for reasons I could not explain. Frau Lungonaso then attempted to insert me into one of my mother's gowns, but I furiously refused, not because I was a hand's breadth too large (though still quite short) or because my mother's taste in formalwear was outdated by many years, but because I would not wear my mother's clothes without her there to lend them to me. Finally, sensing my obstinacy was devolving to hysteria, the woman consented to my second-best gown, two years old and far too small in every direction. So adorned in mediocrity, I stomped outside.

As we approached the entrance to the castle proper, a sudden blast of trumpets startled me, and, tripping over my feet (my hemline could in no way be held responsible), I flailed my way into a puddle.

I sat there, cold sludge seeping into my dress. I could not burst into tears, not before soldiers I had known since birth, and then face the queen with damp cheeks and swollen eyes.

"Get up now," prodded Frau Lungonaso. "Are you sponge or spine?" Whether uttered from cruelty or concern, the woman's words roused my indignation, and I swore to maintain my composure in front of her.

This pathetic situation interested the guards not in the least. Indeed, their backs were to us, their attention focused on the inner courtyard as their hands reflexively checked the straps on their armor and the points of their pikes. "Back to Devil's Bed with them!" hissed one of the men. Again the trumpets within that sanctuary sounded, followed by a great jangling of horsemen. Hastily I lunged away, only just avoiding the flying hooves and rippling black capes. In the fading twilight I could espy the scarlet dragon emblazoned on their chests. Drachensbett! Small wonder the Montagne soldiers whispered curses and checked their weapons twice and thrice.

As the black-clad visitors raced by, a young man—scarcely older than myself, though his armor and frown added years to his face—glanced down at me crouched against the castle wall. His eyes swept across my soiled gown, and then he turned away, speaking to one of his companions as they lashed their mounts across the drawbridge into the streets of Market Town.

It was Frau Lungonaso who recovered first. Perhaps her long-standing position as town gossip had hardened her against surprise. “A bunch of heathens they are,” she sniffed, snapping the mud from her skirts. “You’d best be posting a second watch tonight.”

The nearer guard nodded, too uneasy to question her military directive, and, grunting, helped her pull me to my feet. “And what business have you two in the castle, then?” he asked.

“The queen wants to see Ben,” returned Frau Lungonaso as she brushed mud from my gown and face.

A concerned look passed between the guards. The second man, his face carved deep with grief, stepped closer. “You come from strong stock,” he whispered. “Don’t you forget it, miss.”

“Don’t you forget it, *princess,*” said the other, and dropped his head in a bow.

“Yes, princess,” repeated the second guard, bowing as well. Even Frau Lungonaso, caught up in this impulsive spectacle, dipped into a curtsy.

I had not a single notion how to respond to this unprecedented and utterly unexpected display. Moreover, I feared to speak as I would collapse afresh in tears.

Again, Frau Lungonaso, reverting from attendant to despot, came to my rescue. "Come now," she barked, straightening. "The queen awaits."

As she led me through the grand entrance, the first guard murmured to his partner, "I wish all the fortune in the world to the lass."

"Indeed," said the other sadly. "The poor girl will need every bit."

THREE

If in this narrative I have not yet paid Queen Sophia adequate consideration, particularly given the unrelenting domination the woman would soon claim over every single element of my life, I offer this simple yet honest explanation: for fifteen unbroken years, my mother had toiled to protect me from the woman. It is remarkable, as I reflect upon my childhood, how utterly unaware I was of this situation while it transpired, the truth coming to my notice only in despondent hindsight.

My father and his brother, though raised in the same home by the same loving parents, as adults had selected for wives two women who could not have been less similar. My mother was compassionate, practical, and selfless, devoted to her family and her craft of healing. Her feelings on court intrigue and politics ranged from disinterest to revulsion, and it was at her insistence that our family resided outside the castle proper in the humble yet cozy soldiers' barracks, far from the pomp and pretense of royal life.

Queen Sophia, on the other hand, had arrived as King Ferdinand's bride from her own country, far to the south, cloaked in a haughty aura that even the dimmest resident of Montagne could not but sense. In the two intervening decades, her attitude appeared to have softened only so much as the manners and circumstances of her adopted nation had, in her opinion, improved. The woman took her position more seriously than any royal figure I have ever met, and not only her position but the stipulated position of each member of society, highborn or low, and she treated this ranking and its enforcement as a divinely ordained responsibility.

Had I been a common-born citizen of Montagne, I would have suffered this arrogance no more or less than her next target, but unfortunately I held a unique and highly unenviable position within the kingdom. Sophia, though fastidious in every detail of her queenly role, had failed in one essential and irrevocable way. Despite twenty years of marriage and the ministrations of countless doctors, sages, midwives, and even my mother (over the course of one maddening month that surely tested the last fiber of their patience), the woman had not produced a child.

Thus, in the autumn of the previous year, my parents had been called to a royal council, so formal that even my mother had fretted for days over her meager wardrobe, to be informed that their daughter was now recognized as sole heir to the throne. Indeed, I was expected to move to the castle at once in order to begin a course of instruction, led by Queen Sophia herself, in preparation for my future position. Returning that evening in high dudgeon, my mother declared to my father—not even attempting to lower her voice, such was her indignation—that whatever the fate of Montagne, that harpy would sink her talons into me only over her dead body.

This, precisely, had at last come to pass.

❀ ❀ ❀ ❀

Stumbling now behind Frau Lungonaso across the courtyard, I was presented with yet another flourish of trumpets (the blast sending me fluttering like a barnyard goose) at the castle's great front door.

"Her Royal Highness, the princess," announced Frau Lungonaso, squirreling away every detail for later recounting to any willing set of ears.

The guards, their castle uniforms marked with the black

plumage of mourning, bowed deeply. "Her Royal Highness, the princess," repeated a well-outfitted gentleman (a butler, I later learned) as the great doors swung open. "We shall see to her custody henceforth. Come, Your Highness."

Nose in the air, studiously averting his gaze from my sorry appearance, the man led me down a lengthy corridor, footmen at each closed doorway. The march ended at the entrance to the grand throne room. As we approached, two footmen clothed in black drew open the immense doors. Almost immediately the inner set of doors swung inward.

With a shiver that I could not attribute merely to my soggy skirts, I crept toward the mass of people gathered within. The candelabras, draped with black bunting, hung unlit in reverence for the late king. Black silk covered the queen's throne and the empty king's throne beside it. Sophia sat, her knuckles gleaming white as she gripped her armrests. Two angry red splotches throbbed on her cheeks, contrasting with the purple smudges under her eyes and the pinched white of her mouth. Behind her stood the Privy Council: the counts of our three small counties, the masters of the various guilds, the mayor of Market Town, and sundry lords and ladies in waiting. All wore black, as well as a uniform expression of grim foreboding.

A most awkward silence followed, and with a blush of shame I realized I had not curtsied. Hastily, I did so. I wished now that I had consented to wear my mother's clothing; I felt as ugly as a crust of bread, my shame made all the worse by the queen's visible ire.

Queen Sophia shifted, adjusting her black fur wrap, for though Montagne woolens are celebrated for their velvet hand and gentle drape, she claimed them irritating. "We greet you, Princess Benevolence," she stated emotionlessly, "and offer our condolences for the passing of your mother."

"Thank you," I strangled out.

"We shall, Benevolence, speak with painful frankness, as the situation demands nothing less. Given our recent communication with our neighbor, Drachensbett, we cannot but conclude that this most tragic"—here she, perhaps too dramatically, composed herself—"circumstance, these heinous acts, can be only an act of war."

She paused. The stone-faced solemnity of the men and women arrayed behind her provided no enlightenment or comfort.

"With that in mind, our foremost duty is to protect the throne for the return of Prince—that is, *King* Walter, which he now be. Therefore we shall hold you in our protection to be tutored at long last in the myriad responsibilities and arts of royalty. Should your father not return—a possibility, though tragic, that cannot be discounted—we shall through your alliance of marriage protect Montagne from her voracious foe."

Judging from her expression and those worn by the people behind her, I was expected to speak. But I would need many hours, and an unclouded heart, to decipher this barrage.

Sophia turned to the elderly man at her side. "Is this not true, Lord Frederick?"

"By all means, my lady," he murmured. "I could not have phrased it better."

"Have you any questions of us, Princess?" The queen offered me this as a great favor; with time I would learn how infrequently she solicited my opinion.

"No, Your Majesty," I managed.

"Then you are dismissed, for we have pressing matters of state to which to attend."

As I curtsied, my gown, to my mortification, gave way at last, and the sound of ripping seams reverberated through the hushed room.

The elderly Lord Frederick cleared his throat. "Your Majesty, if I might have leave to escort the princess to her suite . . ."

Queen Sophia frowned. "We consent. But return at once, as we require your counsel."

"By all means, Your Majesty." He stepped forward and offered me his arm.

I am shamed to write that I was too overwhelmed even to accept, so that he was left standing awkwardly, arm ajar, as a lady in waiting tittered.

"Forgive me," he continued, the embodiment of graciousness. "You are too considerate, taking into account the infirmities of an old man. You shall be *my* escort." He slipped his hand around my elbow and led me backwards from the throne room, honoring the queen while shielding my shredded gown from the crowd.

Lord Frederick and I slowly traveled the castle corridors. The gentleman in all honesty was frail, and our pace thus deliberate at best.

"My dearest child, words cannot convey my heartbreak at

your tragedy. Your mother's loss will be mourned throughout this valley." Saying this, the man wiped a tear from his wizened cheek.

I nodded, too overcome to speak. Lord Frederick had been a stalwart member of the Montagne court since at least the time of my grandfather; this I knew. Even more, he had the marvelous ability to pull peppermint drops from my ears, which used to entertain me for hours.

He patted my hand. "Tell me. How may I assist you, Ben?"

I almost wept to hear my name, my real name, spoken within these cold walls. "I'm so confused!" I wailed.

"I understand. As the queen—now queen regent—indicated, the path ahead is shrouded in darkness. The fate of your father, the specter of war . . ."

I grasped the one bit of information that had penetrated my consciousness. "I am really supposed to *marry?*"

"That is the fate of all princesses, my dear. Every storybook teaches it. If it is any consolation, I have heard that such unions may be more than pleasant, even tender."

"But why—why must I live here?" I gestured to the tapestries, the thick stone walls with their deep windowsills.

"The queen would see to your safety. And to your education as well."

"I don't want to be educated!" I stamped my foot.

Lord Frederick spun me about with impressive strength. With a practiced eye he scanned the corridors, then pulled me close. "Your fate, my child, is no longer in your control. You are the embodiment of this kingdom, and if it is to survive the calamities that lie ahead, you must also."

I must have retained an aura of petulance, for he shook me.

"Princess! We hover on the brink of war. Should you have any feelings whatsoever for the people who reside without these walls, accept your lot and consent to Her Majesty's instructions. She knows better than any of us what will be demanded of a queen."

"But I don't want to marry anyone."

"That is not a demand that I, or any of your supporters, would ever make of you."

My head rose. I had supporters?

"However," the old man continued, "you must play this game as the cards are dealt. Bend like the sapling you are. With time we shall find your oaken core."

A sour-faced footman appeared, striding toward us.

Lord Frederick stepped away from me and gestured to the nearest tapestry. "And here, my dear, you see a depiction of your great-, great-, ah, great-grandfather in the War of Three Septembers. The Drachensbett catapults are depicted with remarkable clarity, are they not?"

The lord beamed at me so fiercely that I had no choice but to smile in return. He squeezed my arm.

"Ah," I gulped. "Yes. And the flaming arrows . . ."

His grip relaxed and his face melted into a smile: "I know you will manage brilliantly."

The footman coughed. "My lord, Her Majesty requests your presence."

"Yes, yes. I shall be there presently. Now, my dear, know you the location of your privy chambers? The Peach Rooms, I believe . . ."

So it was that my life passed from the joyous realm of heaven to the choking and inescapable tortures of hell.

FOUR

My privy chambers were without fault. Dubbed the Peach Rooms for the peach-tinted silk of the draperies and walls, they had every accouterment that a young woman of royal blood could possibly desire. The bedroom overlooked the castle's beautiful inner courtyard, Market Town, and on clear days even the far hamlet of Piccolo in the southern foothills. A receiving room, should that young woman wish to entertain guests privately, comprised a balcony roomy enough for three to occupy at their leisure. The library held volumes of novels and etiquette guides, while the dressing room, lined with wardrobes and mirrors, contained more shelves and drawers and storage space than my father's armory, and included an adjoining bath with deep tub. Even the ex–Peach Room connecting the Peach Rooms to the main corridor sported rosebuds and a cozy pink hedgehog.

Once again, I fear, I must interject into the meat of this

narrative some stale crumbs of fact, for the *ex-rooms* would soon occupy—and I pray I do not reveal too much by this intimation—a not insubstantial role in my life. The long-standing legend that giants erected Chateau de Montagne doubtless originated from the truth that the castle walls were thicker than several men standing abreast. Even windows facing the safety of the valley included seats deep enough for a roomy bed, or balconies without need of protrusion from the building's face, so spacious the sill itself.

The interior walls, too, possessed this unique and inexplicable depth. What in another building would be doorway was here broad enough to constitute its own room, with its own name: the "ex-library," "ex-ballroom," "ex–wool storage," "ex-bakery," known by the room to which it led. It took three steps—men's steps, grown men—to pass through an ex-room, and more time still to open and close the doors at each end, such was the walls' thickness.

My father claimed the entire arrangement of ex-rooms stemmed from a need to keep the footmen occupied, which it certainly did, for by tradition the ex-room doors remained closed. Father also pointed out that the ex-rooms constituted a veritable family history, their walls inevitably decorated with variants of the Montagne hedgehog.

As a child, I had always dashed through the ex-rooms, fearful I would accidentally be locked within. This once had happened, or I believed it had, though my mother swore it was only a nightmare, the dim memory clouding my perception. On one visit to the castle, feeling my sweaty grip as we passed from banquet room to corridor, she pulled me aside. "See, Ben? These doors don't even lock—you can open them whenever you want."

"It wasn't these doors," I replied stubbornly. "It was the ex-library."

She smiled. "The ex-library doors don't lock, either. And that was the cabinet, remember?"

I had once managed to lock myself in one of the library's map chests and was ensnared there for some time until an elderly scholar heard my screams. That I had trapped myself while holding a treacle tart only made matters worse, for the maps I did not damage with my frantic kicking I managed to cover in crumbs. Surely I would have suffered some ghastly fate at the hands of Queen Sophia had I not been a blood relation of her husband. As it was, her glare terrified me enough.

However busy the multiple doors kept the footmen, the purpose of the ex-rooms escaped me completely. Only the thickness of the walls could justify their existence, and only giants could explain the wall thickness itself. I knew better than to point this out to my mother, who believed, correctly, that such talk only fed my too active imagination. But my father indulged me by agreeing. Together we invented tales of the giants, who would someday return to the castle from the cloud-veiled reaches of Ancienne.

How frequently did I now dwell on these memories each time I passed through an ex-room to the main corridor, and every reminiscence drove another nail through my heart. The endearing pink hedgehog of my own Peach Rooms pained me most of all; I recognized too well that, for all its charms and the beauty of my new suite, I would have abandoned the entire ensemble without a breath of regret for my own home above the soldiers' barracks.

Yet I could not. I was not permitted even to leave the castle proper for my old residence. This tragedy I learned several days following my arrival, when I managed to slip away from the servants now dressing and feeding and escorting me and made my own way to the castle gates. To my great relief, I recognized the guard Paolo, who had often teased me when I played jacks in the dust of the parade ground.

"And where might you be off to, Your Highness?" he asked, barring my way with a kind look.

"Don't 'Your Highness' me. It's Ben."

"Yes, Your Highness. And what help can we be to you this fine day?"

"I just want to walk about a bit. There are some books I'd like, and . . . little things." I nodded at the barracks.

"You just tell me what you want, now, and I'll bring it back for you, safe and sound," Paolo said in his grandfatherly way.

"You mean that I can't even visit my own home?"

Paolo patted my arm. "It's a job for soldiers now, not fragile young things like yourself. Get back to the castle now, to your own people."

Somehow I held my tears in check until I returned to the privacy of my room, or rather my *rooms,* my new rooms. Then I collapsed. How could Paolo think the queen and her ilk were my people? I had no more relation to them than a pigeon does to a flock of swans—or a vortex of vultures, which the castle's denizens better resembled in both attire and attitude. The ladies in waiting had revealed themselves to be as gossipy and cruel as their reputation, and I avoided them utterly. As for the queen, I had no more interest in her company than in plunging my face into a nest of hornets.

My old life proved just as frustrating. Three friends from

Market Town, girls I had known all my days and who had survived countless scrapes and reprimands with me, trekked up to the castle in their Sunday best to pay their respects to the princess. With trepidation they entered my private receiving room, and their jaws dropped at the sight of plump little Ben now adorned in silken robes, my curls clean and styled. I longed to giggle at their amazement and hug them tight. Soon as I caught sight of them, however, I began to sob with homesickness, and the girls were promptly hustled from my chambers. Learning of this incident, Queen Sophia forbade all further visits, declaring such exhibitions of emotion as highly unsuitable to a girl of my rank. I raged at her cruelty, but the woman's word was law.

In her vigilance, or malice, or cold-heartedness—term it what you will—she barred me even from visiting my mother's grave. "The living require your attention more than the dead," she intoned. "We shall have time aplenty to attend our departed once they are laid properly to rest." As if in compensation, she ordered the masons to present me their plans for my mother's tomb. The block of rose-colored Ancienne stone they had chosen was lovely but anonymous, and the inscription far too grand for such an unpretentious, selfless woman. Even the title crushed me: "Princess Prudence."

Her name was Mother, or Pence; no one spoke of her otherwise. The formality of *Princess* and *Prudence,* the harsh and salivary double *P,* had no relation to the woman who had kissed my tears, assuaged my fears, and through her busy life provided me an unconfined childhood. I had lost my mother in life, and now it appeared I would lose her in death also.

❁ ❁ ❁ ❁

No news, good or ill, came of my father. No Drachensbett messenger arrived bearing ransom note, no woodsman raced to the castle gates with news of a discovery. Every dawn found me pressed to my library window, scrutinizing Ancienne for some sign of him. Soon as the morning rays illuminated the castle courtyard, I moved to the bedroom window, watching for the messenger who would surely arrive with news. More than once I saw my father stumble through the gates, gaunt or injured but beaming in joy at our imminent reunion; when I awoke from these dreams, my heart broke anew.

Whenever possible I would catch the eye of Lord Frederick, imploring him for information, but he routinely turned away. At first I was devastated by these rebuffs, but I soon perceived that the gesture was made not for me but for Sophia. Caution dictated that he display his loyalties to her and her alone, at least in public. When I encountered him in an unguarded corridor, however, he would murmur, "Nothing, I fear," or some such words that at once calmed and broke my heart.

By keeping my tongue still and head low, I overheard many a conversation not meant for my ears, and so learned many facts and tales about the Badger Tragedy, as it was now called, and the fiendish role of Drachensbett. That no man had ever traversed Ancienne did not mean no man *could;* assassins trained in mountaineering might cross in only a few days, lie in wait for their prey, and retrace their route to escape. Indeed, in meeting with the queen after the interment ceremony, the king of Drachensbett had more or less confessed to the crime. Unfortunately I knew no details, for this conversation had apparently been so insulting that the queen forbade all discussion of it.

Learning that the queen's white-lipped anger had little relation to me was some comfort, but still I burned to know how the king had managed to offend so thoroughly my nemesis. Revelation came at last during one of my interminable fittings. When I first moved into the palace, the queen had not bothered to send for my wardrobe (employing that term in its most generous sense) of sturdy wool skirts, stained pinafores, and the thick-soled shoes favored by the mountain people: clothes meant for hard play and great adventures, neither of which was expected of me now. Instead she put her dressmaker to work on gowns suitable for a princess. Gleaming silks, lush brocades, fine laces, and delicate linens went under the blade in my name, though such fabrics had no place on a person of my temperament.

The dressmaker, a sour-faced woman with a mouth forever pinched from years of holding pins, had as little interest in this assignment as did I, but as a loyal servant she diligently attempted to transform a kettle into a cake. Accompanying her were two girls from Market Town who found her bossy impatience a small price to pay for the glamour of castle life. Standing glumly before them, I learned that immobility best prevented pinpricks and chidings, and also that the women soon forgot this dressmaker's dummy had ears of her own.

So it was today. The dressmaker arrived in a particularly foul mood because, I soon ascertained, the queen expected *her,* an artist, a genius with drape and line, the acclaim of every state event, to finish soldiers' uniforms.

"One would think we were going to be attacked tomorrow," the woman sniffed, as though she had unique access to Drachensbett's tacticians.

"Not if their army's scared to cross the mountain!" said one of her assistants, giggling.

The dressmaker's quick scowl shut her up, and the two looked about guiltily. (Such was my status that they did not even glance upward.) Talk shifted to a handsome new chef, and soon enough the dressmaker departed on one of her innumerable trips to the privy, for the woman had a bladder the size of an apricot.

I took advantage of this brief interlude: "What does the Drachensbett army fear?"

As these were the first words I had uttered in ages, the girls jumped like a pair of frogs.

"Please," I pleaded. "Tell me. I beg you."

They eyed each other. "She's got a right, you know," said one. "Besides, remember her mum—how she cured your sister."

"Oh yes," said the other, lighting up. "You should've seen poor Mary, her whole head covered in scabs, big clumps of hair falling out, and pus leaking everywhere—she couldn't sleep lying down, she'd stain the pillow so—"

"What are they afraid of?" I pursued, having no interest in this change of subject.

The girls looked at each other and burst into gleeful laughter. "A dragon!"

"What? Are you saying the Drachensbett soldiers truly believe a dragon lives on Ancienne?"

The first girl—the one without the oozing sister—nodded. "They say that's what did in the king and your ma— "

The girls jerked their attention back to my hemline as the dressmaker reappeared.

Drachensbett blamed my mother's death on a dragon! And not simply country folk whispering stories around a winter fire, but the king himself had the gall to kneel before Queen Sophia on the day after her husband's death—on the afternoon of his interment!—and assert that King Ferdinand had been killed by a fairy-tale creature! Ambush and murder and kidnapping are awful enough, but worse still is veiling such heinous crimes with falsehood. But then, when had Drachensbett ever demonstrated honesty, or nobility? Truly they were an enemy to be despised.

Despised, yes, but also feared. Their awful deeds clearly fit into a grand and cunning scheme to which we in Montagne, the dressmaker not excluded, were patently blind.

Small wonder the queen demanded uniforms for her soldiers and elevated Xavier the Younger to commander, my father's rank. Though it pained me to see the man sporting my father's insignia, now I could understand the reasoning behind it.

Many a night I huddled in my library window, studying the mountain. Where once I had looked for evidence of my father, now I scanned every shadow and ridgeline for enemy movement. Far above my head, I knew, soldiers tramping the parapets watched with as keen an eye, and this knowledge gave me some small comfort. Still, I worried what Drachensbett planned, and why my parents of all people had to suffer their insatiable greed. But I had no one to whom to present my many questions, no one to offer me comfort and reassurance, and so I was left, despondent and alone, to my lessons.

❖ ❖ ❖ ❖

Up to the day of the Badger Tragedy, my hours had been primarily occupied with such rigorous pursuits as poking sticks into holes and covering myself with mud, at both of which I excelled. I knew my letters and numbers of course, and devoured my beloved fairy tales, plodding through more serious work when forced. To be frank, I was young for my age, still playing with dolls when most girls in Montagne had graduated to more serious pursuits, but then, I was not like most girls preparing for lives managing farms and shops and moldy potatoes. Essential work, I grant you, and glad enough would I have been to learn it, the use of moldy potatoes being one of my mother's specialties. In her efforts to shield me from Sophia, however, I had, for better or worse, been kept from such practical education, with little being placed in its stead.

The queen regent—as she now insisted on being addressed—developed an elaborate curriculum designed, so she explained, to produce a pearl of a princess from even a grain of sand such as myself. Her utter disdain for my abilities was tempered by her limitless faith in her own instructional expertise. The lessons she devised included comportment, dance, languages, history, penmanship, needlework, horsemanship, and music. To this day I cannot begin to identify which of them I despised the most.

Much of each day I passed in the company of Lady Beatrix, a tall and bony woman of unknowable age who never appeared without a wig and a thick spackling of powder, rouge, and lipstick, a mole painted somewhere between her cheekbone and chin depending on the formality of the occasion. As an educator, she was utterly lacking.

Her notion of history centered on genealogy, emphasizing Queen Sophia's superior bloodlines. Though she spoke several languages, her vocabulary consisted of fashion and dining terms and fawning, useless phrases. Because she insisted on teaching me three tongues at once, I eventually uttered such nonsense as "the draperies in this hall are lovely," but in a tangle of languages and grammar that not even she could unravel. Penmanship I found equally wretched, for I had far less interest in the appearance of my words than in their substance, a concept that held no meaning for my teacher. Gladly would I have returned to my task of recipe transcription, but such practical work was now denied me.

My friends from Market Town, on learning the queen forbade their visits, set about corresponding instead. As these letters were presented in the presence of Lady Beatrix, she insisted that my replies employ "the palace tongue," as she phrased it. She would, moreover, dictate my responses so that I might familiarize myself with the ornate and gauzy drivel of formal court communication. Needless to say, my correspondents' interest soon faded as their heartfelt questions and familiar anecdotes were answered with simpering generalities.

Needlework—oh, hateful needlework! How many

loathsome hours did I spend embroidering handkerchiefs with ridiculous flowers and illegible initials, only for Beatrix to reject them. "Someday," she would simper, "a prince himself will request your handkerchief as token. This would be shameful to present."

"I don't care about tokens!" I snapped. "I don't care about princes, either!" I found it effortless to talk back to her, but ultimately unsatisfying, as she ignored me utterly.

"Remember, Benevolence," she would say, handing me another square of linen, "'Tis a needle, not a lance. Gentle stitches."

Dance and music were taught by stout little Monsieur Grosbouche, whose hands were as cold and damp as freshly caught fish. He, too, believed that the promise of well-born bachelors should inspire my greatest exertions. As he dragged me through each minuet, polonaise, and gavotte, puffing the beat with odiferous breath, I entertained myself by stepping on the wide bows of his high-heeled dance slippers, then sweetly awaiting his stumble.

Astoundingly, he never identified my role in the unruliness of his laces. As with Lady Beatrix, who sat at the harpsichord banging through the same handful of songs, he believed my inherent clumsiness, not my wits, left him with aching ankles at the end of every class.

I shall not describe my attempts at violin.

Horsemanship, such as it was, consisted of being led sidesaddle around the inner courtyard. However longingly I gazed through the gates, I could never pass to Market Town and the countryside beyond, for the guards kept me under close watch and I had not skill to bribe or bully my way past them. Chateau de Montagne held me as tightly as an acorn holds its nut.

Of all these dreadful lessons, comportment may have been the worst. This vague title included not only the most graceful ways to curtsy and walk (versus my routine stumbling, particularly on stairs) but also table manners. A Montagne breakfast consists of a simple soft roll with hot chocolate, or hot cider for adults. Yet I ripped my roll like a savage, slurped my drink, dribbled jam, shed crumbs . . . No matter how sincere my efforts, the litany droned on without respite. Eventually I surrendered all effort and returned to my baser instincts.

Unless the queen was occupied with state business, she demanded I accompany her to dinner, ostensibly to honor my position but in reality to watch my every gesture and mention its fault. Lady Beatrix, though we outranked her, often joined us so that the two women could demonstrate with each other the most fitting conversation and eating habits.

I resented every moment of these meals. What was the point of dainty bites, feigning lack of hunger when actually famished, or delight in food that lacked all seasoning? And, worst of all, why was I never permitted to eat my fill? I spent the evenings in a misery of starvation, my stomach stating what my mouth could not, and watching longingly as footmen removed Beatrix's half-touched meal.

"A queen does not concern herself with the trivialities of nourishment," Sophia would state, hearing my belly's growl. "Her attention need be focused elsewhere. My dear Lady Beatrix, does your plate suit you?"

"By all means, Your Majesty," Beatrix groveled. "And may I praise this most excellent menu. The items so complement each other."

I stared miserably down at my dish, watching the beets mingle with an unidentifiable green sauce that covered the small, overcooked lamb chop. Ghastly it looked, and ghastly it tasted as well, but such was my hunger that I consumed every morsel.

"Indeed they do, Lady Beatrix, and we commend your keen eye. We have always enjoyed the gracious balance of color on a plate."

Never once, in all the years I knew her, did the queen employ the first-person singular. Oh, how I raged at her pompous assumption that she could speak for the entire kingdom, in particular for *me*. She had no idea what passed through my head; the fact that it remains attached to my neck proves this. Every time she opened her mouth, I would reflexively stiffen in anticipation of her next pompous assertion.

❀ ❀ ❀ ❀

My frustration with my situation deepened as the summer progressed. In the tumult following the Badger Tragedy, the queen often mentioned my father, and took pains to emphasize that as regent she held the throne solely in expectation of his return. But as no word or sign of him came, her shrewdly worded declarations grew more infrequent, her silence quieting the entire court, until it was as if he had never existed. The throne of the king of Montagne she ordered fitted with a black tasseled shroud, and this embellishment declared as effectively as a proclamation that she expected no man ever to replace or even to join her. Though I ached to see my father alive, as the cycle of planting and harvest passed outside the castle walls, I would have been grateful even for word of tragedy, so long as some word arrived. But none did.

In those first miserable months, my sole source of joy came from a hamper of food I would find hidden beneath my bed. Nestled inside would be raisin buns wrapped in warm napkins, a fruit tart, a steaming pitcher of chocolate. Who delivered it, I never learned, but I cannot begin to describe the comfort it provided, the knowledge that someone in that stony edifice took the time and risk to provide me this glorious consolation.

I wept as I huddled in my nightdress, gulping down these treats. The food brought back almost unbearable memories of a happier time, and its warmth provided a physical comfort that the soft July evenings could not begin to supply. Sated at last, I would conceal the basket again, careful to gather every incriminating crumb.

At times the hamper appeared nightly; at other periods, not for several days. But the knowledge of this secret preserved me from the queen's endless and tasteless dinners, and her bullying as well.

❀ ❀ ❀ ❀

This, in a nutshell, was my life following my father's disappearance and my mother's death. Any sane and compassionate soul would define such an existence as intolerable. So, too, did I recognize that some modification had to occur, and soon, to change this cheerless state of affairs.

The situation did change. It got worse.

FIVE

My downfall, inevitably, was triggered by food. Please understand that in those first months, however dire my situation might appear, I never approached starvation. The traditional three meals were served me each day, supplemented by tea with Monsieur Grosbouche at the conclusion of every dance lesson, and at times a small cake or other delicacy for infrequent state events.

But never once, excepting my secret hamper, did I eat to the point of satiation, a sensation I had experienced constantly in my former life and that I missed almost as profoundly as my mother's embrace. Within my first hours in Chateau de Montagne, Queen Sophia made clear her feelings on my appearance. "We are not beggars at banquet," she announced, observing me at our first dinner together. Often she would order the footmen to serve me a half-portion, demanding I finish no sooner than did she, and the woman ate at the pace of a dripping icicle. "A princess," she would proclaim, "requires a graceful and willowy carriage, not the appetite of a swineherd."

Yet however restricted my servings, I never thinned, this truth made all the more obvious when my dresses, prepared on the expectation that I would soon fit them, continued to rip seams and pop buttons. The queen watched my every forkful with a hawk's eye, calculating how such paltry servings could maintain me. I am sure my smug acceptance of her restrictions only increased her suspicions. She was a cunning adversary, and had I been wiser I would have known to present an abject façade. Alas, I did not.

So it came to pass that one afternoon I was summoned from dance class. Delighted as I was to escape clam-fisted Monsieur Grosbouche, I knew Sophia's demand for my presence could only bode ill. I dawdled my way to the throne room, then curtsied before her.

"Dear Benevolence," the queen began, with a measured tone I had learned could mask any emotion, "we grow concerned that you have not sufficient regard for your position." A version of this statement I endured almost daily; she could be speaking of any number of infractions. "Your childish passions, while unchecked under others' care, must within these walls be controlled, or the nation shall suffer."

With effort I unclenched my fists at her insult of my mother.

"Tell us, dear Benevolence, do you yet indulge in unnecessary foodstuffs?"

"I follow Your Majesty's guidance always." I curtsied again.

"We are pleased to hear it. We fear, however, that you yet succumb to primitive urges." She flourished my secret hamper. "Is this not familiar to you?"

Heart hammering, I did my best to project an expression of mild puzzlement. "I do not believe so, Your Majesty."

To my astonishment, the queen merely nodded. "We shall attend to this matter presently. For the time being, you must return to your lessons. We are told your progress is quite remarkable."

"As you wish, Your Majesty," I replied, and plodded back to the ballroom. My unease grew at the conclusion of dance class, when with a scurrying of footmen Sophia herself appeared in the ballroom, flustering Monsieur Grosbouche so completely that for once our fumbling errors were not my fault alone.

"Accompany us, dear Benevolence," she stated as Monsieur Grosbouche nigh toppled over in his passionate bowing. Exiting the ex-ballroom, she gestured to her left. "We shall stroll together to your quarters."

"Your Majesty, if I may be so bold, I believe my suite lies in the direction opposite."

"We shall see" was all she replied. She swept along, artfully moving her skirts with one hand. Yet the northwest corner of the castle held naught but her apartment. Where, pray tell, were we going?

At the entrance to her privy chambers, two footmen bowed stiffly, opening the doors to her gilded ex-room. I could not suppress a shiver: was she intending us to *share* a room?

Inside the queen's private reception room, a servant girl curtsied.

"Is it prepared for us?" Sophia demanded.

"Yes, Your Majesty," the girl squeaked, remaining bent before us—as much to avoid interaction as to demonstrate fealty, I suspected.

The reception room itself could not fail to dazzle me. Lush couches and delicate tables filled every corner, and the walls were draped with the gold-threaded tapestries that

Sophia had brought to Montagne from her native lands. It was whispered that Sophia's grandmother had spun the golden threads from straw itself, though the tale remained shrouded in mystery, the queen refusing to discuss it.

As handsome as these chambers were, however, I preferred my own little rooms with their pale peach curtains and simple library. Little did I know.

The queen strode to a door so diminutive I never would have paid it notice. Opening it, she revealed a space as dark and foreboding as the underworld itself. "Benevolence, we would that you led."

I crept forward. Compared to the richness of the queen's rooms, the narrow closet appeared all the gloomier. Near paralyzed with fear, Sophia's glare upon me, I realized with a start that I was entering not a compartment but a staircase of sorts, built into the castle walls, with sides of rock and treads carved of stone.

With great trepidation I began to ascend, relieved for once to hear the queen behind me, as I did not want to occupy this narrow darkness alone. The wall itself must have been circular, for the staircase bent forever to the left as we climbed the rough steps, the queen staying well back of my errant heels.

At last, feeling as though I were atop Ancienne herself, I struck a barrier of wood.

"You may open it," the queen instructed.

In the dim light I discerned a pallet with a worn coverlet. In truth, it was not much humbler than what I had known as a child, but I noted acutely its contrast to my plush bed several floors below. An empty basin built into the wall and a chamber pot (with cover, thankfully) completed the décor. The stone floor had no carpets to warm it, the walls no tapestries. As we entered, a quick scrabbling—the room, being round, had no corners—revealed the presence of mice. At least, I prayed they were mice. Rats I could not tolerate. Unlike those of the castle below, these stone walls offered little respite from the summer heat, and the atmosphere hung close and sour, for the room clearly had not been aired in many years, and a recent sweeping had filled the air with dust. A cell it was indeed.

The queen stood for a moment, inspecting my new quarters and, I am certain, catching her breath from the climb. "We are pleased," she uttered at last. "We pray the princess shall use this opportunity to reflect on her newfound responsibilities. Would you not agree, Benevolence?"

I longed to ignore her, but the woman's power, as she so

brutally demonstrated, far exceeded my own, and oppressive though the room was, it was not a dungeon. Not yet. "Yes, Your Majesty," I answered without emotion.

"Are you not grateful for this opportunity?"

"Yes, Your Majesty." I dropped into a curtsy to avoid meeting her eyes.

"Beatrix and her staff shall arrive presently to dress you for dinner. In the weeks to come, we shall be delighted to hear of your developments in restraint." With that, Sophia swept from the room. The door closed behind her with an ominous creak, followed by the final sharp click of a lock.

❀ ❀ ❀ ❀

As I had climbed the stone staircase more than half convinced I was en route to my execution, my initial reaction involved a fair measure of relief, for a sliver of pie is better than naught. The blankets on the pallet, worn though they were, appeared at least clean. With effort I released the corroded window latch, and the tumble of warm fresh air reminded me that all was not lost.

As I dwelled upon the matter, however, I began to understand the true wretchedness of my situation. My farsighted ancestors had erected Chateau de Montagne at the seam, as it were, where Ancienne's gentle eastern slopes meet its vertical northern cliffs. The Peach Rooms I had been given upon my arrival to the castle overlooked lovely Montagne, and the mysterious and imposing richness of Ancienne, her skirts patterned with crofters' cottages, apple orchards, grain fields, and the snowy sheep that produce our noted woolens. This new room, however—and I am most generous in my use of the term "room," for it was much closer to a cell—had one window, of smallish dimensions, that faced north. Instead of fertile valley, I could see only the torrent of the Great River, the switchbacks built into the cliff far below, and the distant foreign mountains. I occupied, in fact, the castle's tallest tower, which explained the stifling heat that radiated from the cell's southwestern walls.

I mulled on the tower-bound princess whose lover employed her hair as rope. My own curly locks—one of my better features, I will admit, *better* being a relative term—hung just past my shoulders, and barely draped over the windowsill. At this height, I would require leagues of hair and a scalp like a pachyderm's to support it. Besides, I reflected, scowling, I did not want a man coming to *me*. I instead required a means of departure.

But that would be impossible. The queen now controlled

my every move; I would eat, and dress, and depart this cell at her pleasure. Not one soul in the kingdom, certainly not the timid servant girl who cringed before Sophia, would have courage enough to find this cell and slip me food. Any illusions I retained that my life might be my own were gone forever.

In the weeks that followed I suffered greatly, though some kind souls did extend small offerings. At dinner one night I found a raisin roll hidden in my napkin. Discreet as I sought to be, Queen Sophia must have sensed my delight, and by the following night she replaced the dining staff. Occasionally I would discover a sweet tucked inside my writing book, or on taking the hand of a footman I would find a small wedge of chocolate in my own. But all in all, her noose grew ever tighter.

The situation collapsed completely at dinner one September evening. Perhaps it was the full moon that drove me to madness, or the gnawing, relentless emptiness of my heart. Whatever the trigger, the powder had been well packed, and my explosion, though shocking, was not altogether unexpected.

As always, the queen and Lady Beatrix prattled. The queen dined in a gown of poppy red silk laced with gold, the fabric's unearthly shimmer reflecting the queen's own serpentine nature. Intent on eating with sufficient restraint that my portion not be further reduced, I ignored my companions as best I could, speaking only when addressed directly. As the second course, a bland pork loin baked in pastry, was laid before us, my stomach rumbled.

Lady Beatrix tittered. "Forgive me, Your Majesty. I am unused to this earthiness."

"We do better to rise above such vulgarity," the queen admonished her lady while I seethed. How dare they describe me as vulgar, as if my belly's grumbling were within my control! Yet I set my jaw, determined not to reveal my aggravation.

At last the queen nodded for our plates to be cleared. Lady Beatrix, I could not but notice, had barely touched her food. "Your Majesty," I spoke, "forgive me, but I worry at the distress the chef must experience to see his labor slighted so."

The queen glared at me. "How often each night must we instruct you that we do not dwell on food?"

"Well," I retorted, the devil at last possessing me completely, "some of us do!" With that, I leaned across the table, snatched up Lady Beatrix's tart, and stuffed it into my mouth.

My efforts at mastication aside, time appeared to stop,

though when I finally swallowed—the pork, being tough as well as bland, required no minor amount of exertion—I could discern the ticking of the great clock behind me. Beatrix, and the staff as well, observed me with silent horror.

Again the queen sighed. "For some time we have anticipated such a transgression from those who were never taught to control their basest instincts. Arise, Benevolence."

Still swallowing bits of tart, I did so. Sophia motioned to a footman. "Hold her right hand steady. We would not have her flinching."

"I flinch at nothing!" I proclaimed, remembering my brave soldier father. I resolved to do him honor, wherever he might be, and I boldly flourished my hand.

The queen's eyebrows rose, but she said nothing. Instead, standing, she pulled from some hidden pocket a short leather strap, and, setting her jaw, began at once to beat my palm.

The pain was extraordinary. It took every fiber of my being not to snatch my hand away, cram my burning fingers into my mouth, and run sobbing from the room. I bit my lip, trying to think of my mother, of summer days, of soft kittens and fairy tales.

Finally she halted. With a heartfelt sigh, I commenced to sit.

"We are not finished, Princess. Turn your hand, if you please."

Again, with control I did not know I possessed, I held out my hand, palm down. Immediately as the lashes fell welts began to form. My fingers, swollen already, grew pink and then deep red. When after a seeming eternity the beating ended, I did not move, so desperate was I to deny that this inflamed and agonizing appendage was actually attached to my person.

Readjusting the train to her gown, the queen settled herself. "How courteous of you, Benevolence," she said, lifting her wineglass, "to await those of higher rank."

I eased into my chair. For a moment my fury blocked the anguish. Soon as I moved, however, the pain returned in force.

The meal continued. For some time no one conversed, as Sophia's focus was elsewhere and no one, of course, may speak before the queen.

Determined not to display any suffering, I struggled as best I could with knife and fork. The queen, I noticed, consumed three glasses of wine rather than her usual one. Occasionally a true emotion would cross her face, escaping that icy façade. And the emotion I saw most frequently—or that I chose to so interpret—was disappointment. I had not been broken.

This realization gave me the strength to survive that interminable dinner.

At last the footmen cleared the roast and presented each of us a small cake, frosted and gilded until it resembled a precious porcelain ornament. From experience I knew that however lovely the exterior, the center would be as dry and tasteless as old wood, and that the entire dessert could better serve as doorstop than victuals. But beggars cannot select their sauces, and well did I recognize that my next meal would not come for many hours. Taking the daintiest, gentlest (for breaking this crust was no mean feat) forkful that I could manage, I began to eat.

Across the table, the queen and Lady Beatrix continued their useless dialogue. The queen, I noticed, had two bright circles of color in her cheeks, and Beatrix, following her mistress's lead on wine consumption as on all matters, spoke more piercingly than usual.

Sophia turned to me. "Benevolence, you must join us. Insignificant as our conversation may seem, a queen's greatest responsibility is to learn the art of speaking well while saying nothing."

"Forgive me, Your Majesty," I replied docilely. "But I was taught that a queen's greatest responsibility is to bear her husband a child."

A veritable broadsword of silence crashed down upon the room.

Queen Sophia folded her napkin and placed it at her side. "Your left hand, please."

By the time this strapping ended, we were both of us visibly wheezing, mightily as we tried to hide it. The effort of eliciting a cry—unsuccessful, I am proud to relate—had raised beads of perspiration on Sophia's upper lip. I myself bit my cheek so strongly that I tasted blood. Finished, we returned to our seats, dabbing our mouths with our napkins as though attending to a drop of gravy. As no one else survives to bear witness, allow me to aver that I was as ladylike in this gesture as Queen Sophia herself.

Finally, following ices and cordials, the queen rose. Lady Beatrix and I obediently followed. Without a word the queen left the banquet hall. As had become our practice, I accompanied her, for she alone could admit me to my "room."

Normally as we walked the corridors together, the queen would point out the failures she had not had opportunity to mention during the meal itself: I clinked my water glass against my wine; I thanked the footmen too heartily; and, always, I did not join the conversation. Tonight, however, she did not speak once. Word of our struggle—of my beating, to be frank—must have galloped through the castle, for footmen stood frozen to hear every word. Alas, there was none.

Within the queen's apartment, her young maid cowered, acutely aware of the unearned scolding she would doubtless soon receive. Unable to open the stairwell door with my swollen hands, I had to wait, curtsying, for the queen. She flung it open and preceded me up the stairs, puffing visibly. Moonlight flooded my cell, and in the light I could observe Sophia's chest heaving with effort. Normally she wished me good night, though with enough coldness to cancel the courtesy. Tonight, however, she did not speak but only slammed shut the door with a resounding clang.

My sobs drowned out the click of the lock. Alone at last, I collapsed, clutching my miserable hands as I had longed to all night. I had not water, even, to bathe them! My battle with the queen had taken every particle of my strength. I could not repeat it—could not even bear the thought. And yet she would sit as regent for years to come, until I reached my majority, the particulars of which she alone had power to determine. Should she wish, I could remain under her cold and bloodless thumb for a decade or more. I was alone—completely, utterly, bitterly alone, barely able to bend my aching digits. My mother was dead, murdered by our enemies as part of some oblique master plan; my father, wherever he be, showed no sign of returning. Even Lord Frederick, so solicitous on my first dismal day in this place, had departed for points abroad, his return date undetermined. It was I, a plump and heartbroken girl, aligned against a woman who had every indication of being Satan himself.

I sobbed for I do not know how long. No matter how I prayed, no fairy godmother appeared. No elf or leprechaun or world-weary wizard materialized to provide the secret weapon against my foe. I remained alone in a mouse-infested cell, empty but for a pallet and the nightdress into which I now had to struggle.

Getting into the nightdress was not to be the problem; it was struggling out of my gown that overwhelmed me. Normally a handmaid arrived following the queen's departure to unfasten my layers and attend to my corset and stockings. She would then, under the queen's orders, take my eveningwear with her on the absurd assumption that I might escape my tower, and the further absurd assumption that, once escaped, I would object to being seen in my nightclothes.

Tonight, however, I was alone. The queen must have forbidden her from attending me or the maid had sense enough to avoid Sophia's fury. Either way, I heard no tread to indicate I would soon be released. Exhausted to my core, I craved sleep. But even if my fingers had worked, I could not have removed the constricting and obstinate garb in which I had been clad.

Utterly defeated, I lay my head against the cold stone wall of my prison and sobbed anew. Moonlight cast a daunting sliver of shadow across the floor, but I paid it no heed. I craved only resolution. Even death, harsh as this may sound, seemed apt. Then I might join my mother in the afterlife. I lay my aching hands on the wall, intent to push off, to move to the window and leap out. And then—

The wall beneath my left hand gave way. It did not collapse, should that image come to mind. Instead, it simply, in that instant, abandoned all pretext of solidity.

In the many years since this one unforgettable moment, I have struggled to explain this experience, how best to convey its utterly terrifying *foreignness*. Imagine descending a staircase. Arriving at the bottom, you confidently stride forward—but you have miscalculated. Another step remains, and instead of touching solid floor you flail through the air for a life-saving handhold. And though you fall only two hand breadths at most, the terror of that one helpless moment remains, poisoning your consciousness, for some time afterward.

Such was my sensation. Moreover, I did not suffer it on a staircase, where one has experience with such momentary crises, but against a solid rock wall.

I leapt back in horror, my heart in my throat. What had I felt? In the moonlight I could perceive clearly the wall's rough stones, with the same mass and substance as the mountain itself. In fact, in the nocturnal illumination their origin was obvious, for Ancienne stone always glitters slightly.

I must be mad. My hands were damaged, obviously. I knew not what I felt.

Sheepishly I stepped forward. I touched the spot where my head had rested. In the most literal sense, it was rock solid. My right hand continued along the wall. Inflamed as my fingers were, the rock registered in unique and painful ways, all of them substantial. With great care, I reached out my left hand, still throbbing from the beating. I touched rock

. . . rock again . . . and then before my disbelieving eyes, my arm plunged to the elbow into the stone.

Again I leapt back. I examined my arm. Except for the beating, it appeared normal. But hands do not penetrate rock!

Determined now, I slapped the masonry. But my fingers touched nothing—perhaps at best the skimming effect of silk; certainly not stone. Again my arm disappeared to the elbow. With enormous control, panting with effort, I held it there in place, suppressing panic at the sight of my absent limb. Deliberately I moved my arm. It moved—it moved as an arm should move. The space, solid as it appeared, *felt* empty. I brought my right hand over and slipped it in until my other arm, too, was elbow-deep in solid stone.

Not daring to breathe, I dragged both arms to one side. Almost at once they hit a vertical barrier, undetectable to my eyes. My fingers slipped down this smooth impediment, which felt for all the world like a doorjamb. Up I continued, until standing on my toes I felt a "lintel" (so I dubbed it) above my head. No visible sign, however—rock and masonry had no relation to this smooth, tactile solidity. Dizzy with confusion and exhilaration, I ran my rock-bound arms along this lintel, swirling them about. Almost at once I located the other side of the doorjamb. There. I had found three sides of a doorway, as cleverly disguised as a moth on a tree. I stood, a swollen hand out of sight on each side of this mysterious and baffling portal.

My pulse rang in my ears. Cautiously, as a swimmer tests the waters, I extended my foot, still in its beribboned dinner slipper. The stone engulfed my shoe and ankle, the hem of my gown disappearing into the stone.

The ground on the other side felt solid.

What had I to lose? Who would miss me, should this end in tragedy?

With a deep breath, I stepped through.

Part Two

In which I make

several unusual discoveries

SIX

Coward that I am, I squeezed my eyes shut, and so experienced intensely the sensation of cool silk. Finding myself on the far side of the portal, puffing in relief at the stone beneath my feet, I forced one eyelid open. Before my nose was another wall of stone. Reaching out, I touched rough-hewn masonry and crudely applied mortar, all blanketed with the dust of age. In fact, excepting the dust it matched exactly the walls of the staircase from the queen's reception room to my cell. With a jolt, I realized that just as that horrid stair occupied the tight space between two walls, so did this most peculiar roomlet.

Dim moonlight filtered through the secret portal. On the far side of the doorjamb my cell and bed appeared clear as day. As I peered about the roomlet's gloaming, I espied an ascending flight of steps built between the walls, so matched in appearance and construction to the staircase from the queen's reception room to my cell that without question they had been constructed by the same hand. Yet *whereto* did this flight lead? My tiny cell occupied the highest floor of the highest tower of Chateau de Montagne. Above was naught but slate roofing and sky.

For some time I chewed my lip. It made some sort of sense—should something as irrational as this experience ever be labeled *sensible*—that a doorway such as this would lead to a secret corridor, and what else is a staircase but a corridor improved by elevation? The dusty little roomlet in which I now stood otherwise served as no more than well-disguised closet. Dearly might an emperor or Midas pay for a closet so perfectly hidden from spies and thieves, but it had no purpose in a barren cell. No, doorway and staircase were but a conduit to the unknown.

I had come this far. I began to climb.

Within a half-dozen steps, the sparse moonlight dissipated so completely that I was ascending in total darkness. Timidly I probed and tested each step and riser before settling my weight. Swollen and aching though my fingers were, still they swept the jagged stones, verifying the solidity of my surroundings. Ever higher I mounted. Then my vision, overwhelmed with strain, began to mislead me, for steps and walls, ghostly in a pale white light, appeared. I turned my head upward, and my heart froze, for light—ever stronger and whiter—drifted down from above.

Though I stood as a statue for some time, my ears ringing with the effort of my concentrated listening, I could discern no footstep or rustle, no indication that the space above was occupied by a human . . . or other presence. Again gathering my scanty resolve, I resumed my creeping journey.

Mounting the last steps, I could now make out a tiny chamber, as neatly designed as a cut gem, tucked beneath the conical roof of the tower. Strong moonlight poured through four diminutive dormer windows, as though the round panes of glass had magnified the faint beams tenfold. Just as a lighthouse via mirrors and lenses transforms the flame of a single candle into a powerful beam, so, too, apparently, did these windows work with moonlight: a lighthouse turned in upon itself.

In this enchanted light I perceived a space such as I had never known. Odd cabinets with peculiar locks lined the walls. A cobwebbed mirror hung above a workbench blanketed in a jumble of unidentifiable objects. A lectern displaying an open book, an unlit candelabra to one side, stood in the room's center. Every item—I cannot emphasize this strongly enough—was shrouded in dust more than a finger width deep, accented by bird droppings powdery with age; bird nests crumbled in the turret's peak. Mice had left an otherworldly maze of trails on the floor, which was so thick with dust that it felt as soft as carpet.

I stole toward the lectern, small eddies of dust rising about my ankles. Once arrived, I had another fright, for the mighty tome resting there, though obviously ancient with its yellowed pages and aged leather binding, was as clean as the queen's own throne. Thick dust draped every adjoining surface, and bird droppings as well (I was revolted to note), but the book itself lay pristine.

With effort, I calmed myself. There were no footprints in the room, no evidence of occupancy for a century or more. The book itself must have some mysterious power. Inadvertently I proved this when, in reaching to touch the binding, a thick clump of dust dropped from my sleeve. The dust drifted downward as dust is wont to do, but as it neared the book, it purely and simply vanished. How clever! I scooped up a large handful of dust to test this again but at the last moment refrained, sensing (and I shall forever look upon this moment as a great leap in my maturity) that perhaps a volume of such antiquity and obvious capability should not be put to use for parlor tricks.

Those childhood tales of the founding of Montagne, the legendary couple who cured the mountain giants' chilblains and through magic protected their new country from harm . . . those fictions, I suddenly realized, must have some foundation in fact. Magic alone could explain my passage through a solid masonry wall, and magic alone explained the presence, and certainly the contents, of this secret room. Why I of all people would stumble upon this lost and forgotten chamber at this particular moment in time; that I could not explain. Except—and this realization sent me gasping so deeply that I spent several minutes coughing dust from my lungs—except for the fact that I, as granddaughter of the king, had descended directly from Montagne's founders. However many generations later, their blood flowed in my veins. This marvelous adventure was, in some manner, my birthright.

Again I peered at the spotless open book. After wiping one aching hand on my gown (which, sadly, was already far more soiled than brocade should ever be), I reached out a trembling finger and touched it.

I did not disappear. That was a blessing. The book felt clean to my touch, of course, but otherwise booklike. When I tried to turn the page, however, my eyes grew wide, for however papery the pages felt and appeared, with their tiny words and inked drawings, the book remained as solid and immovable as a block of granite.

If I had not yet come to the conclusion that this tome was a force of magic, the title words—difficult to discern, for the room though illuminated by the moon had not light for scholarship—left no doubt. "The Elemental Spells," they proclaimed, in a flowing, archaic script I would discover soon enough was not the easiest to decipher. A dense paragraph followed, too challenging to read in the weak light, and then a series of precise illustrations and captions, with arrows highlighting specific elements, much as a cookery book might demonstrate the proper way to trim a roast, or an engineering manual the ideal configuration of a gristmill.

The pictures greatly intrigued me. Each showed a pair of hands gesturing in a most specific manner. A sketch of a hand with snapping fingers, for example, emphasized that the snap should be off the third, or ring, finger. I attempted this. My own fingers were so swollen that I could scarce manipulate them, yet, consumed with curiosity, I forced them to bend.

With great effort I produced a small sound, nothing akin to the well-known snap with which we are all of us familiar, but noise nonetheless in that silent room. Beneath this drawing was a series of words in a tongue I did not recognize; it looked wild, foreign, and unpronounceable. Helpfully, a second line of text sounded the words out syllable by syllable. With great focus I whispered the words, though I had not a clue in the world what such gibberish would produce.

Again I spoke, uttering the words with more confidence now, and at the same time forcing my fingers into their snap. At once a minuscule puff of flame appeared in my palms. I shrieked—well would anyone, I should say, under such tension—and leapt backwards. Breathless with alarm, I rubbed my hands, searching out a burn. There was none, naught beyond the welts and grime already present.

However unscathed I was for now, caution dictated I attend more closely. I returned to the book. The next illustration was of two hands cupped; another sequence showed the hands working in unison through an elaborate snap and fluttering move. Once burned, as it were, I now doubled my vigilance, and practiced the nonsensical words with my arms held straight out from my sides, fingers stiff and wide to avoid any possible misunderstanding.

Across the two pages, I could see now, every chain of pictures ended with cupped hands, and each set of hands held a different substance. One clutched a lump resembling soil, another water with rippling surface. The third pair held what could only have been fire, sans a single indication of discomfort. The last hands I puzzled over, for they appeared to harbor a puff of mist, much like the clouds forever swirling about the base of our waterfall. These pictures meant *something,* I knew, but what?

Suddenly, as I scanned the pages' title, it struck me. The *elemental spells* these were, and such they produced: the four elements of earth, water, fire, and air.

What good such spells would accomplish I had not a clue. The ability to make dirt, or air, seemed rather a waste of magic. Fire, however, particularly a flame one could hold without danger—that was a different situation altogether. I made another attempt at the hand gestures, enunciating as clearly as possible and struggling to align properly my words and movements. Finishing, I gripped my two hands together, determined to cup the flame for a moment at least.

My palms filled with a brilliant glow as flames lapped upward. Reflexively I jerked back my head, afraid my curls might catch fire. But I felt not a hint of pain. The fire, in fact, soothed my inflamed skin. Hardly daring to breathe, I lifted this magical fire to my face. I blew on it. The flames danced as flames will, burning more brightly still. Marveling at this miracle, I noticed the dust-caked candelabra and the drooping, mouse-gnawed candles. Careful to hold my fire out of harm's way, I blew dust from the curled wicks. This could not work—and yet, when I held my flame close, the first wick caught with ease. The room brightened as the candle flame grew. Thrilled beyond measure, I lit the remaining candles, and this warm yellow glow mingled with the pure white moonlight to suffuse the room with brightness. The page before me now read clearly, and, emboldened by my success, I set to work deciphering the tight prose.

This, too, took time, as the writer's spelling was creative at best, his phrasing archaic, and his penmanship, lovely though it appeared, lacked that crucial element of legibility. Halfway through the first sentence, I was already cursing him—or her, I should say in fairness, for the script, with its elaborate flourishes and illuminations, did have a feminine quality. With the greatest effort, I made my way through the first paragraph, which consisted of a series of warnings, the most important being that the spells could not be used for profit, that the manufacture of ice presented unique challenges and might result in frostbite, and that attempts at flight would require additional spell work. The warning against profiteering included a most disturbing sketch of a man fabricating a large crystal, only to lose his hands. It had never occurred to me that "earth" might include gems and metals. Even so, wealth held little appeal. Far more interested was I in the concept of flight. Is that what the warning meant, that one produced the element of air in order to *fly?* To fly like a . . . like a witch, on a broom? My mind reeled.

I spent the rest of the night in practice. Lucky I was that my first attempt had been so successful, else I would have forsaken the effort entirely. Try as I might, I could not construct air, not even a puff. My attempts at earth were equally futile. Perhaps I managed a dozen grains of soil, but my hands by this point were so filthy that I could not separate old dirt from new. Furious at my imbecility, I returned to my one success and produced a flame so powerful that it singed my hair. With a yelp I dropped the fire, snuffing it, and studied again the minuscule printing, only to learn that emotion played as strong a role in these spells as speech or gesture. I could control the volume, and to a certain extent the contents (specifying the type of earth, say, or that dangerous ice), with my mind. The writer further explained, as if reading my thoughts, that self-control was the very foundation of spell work. I could not resist a heartfelt snort. At the moment I had far too many critics of my self-control; I did not need another.

Nonetheless, I paid close attention to my mood, ignoring the stench of burnt hair. If I could not manage earth or air, perhaps I might at least produce water. This, too, required great concentration. At one point my hands grew damp, which I considered a great victory. Reinvigorated, I wiped my palms on my dress, leaving two long black smears across my middle. My swollen fingers ached, growing stiffer with every movement I forced from them. Finally, after what must have been the twentieth attempt, I again clasped my cupped hands together and to my astonishment found them brimming.

"Oh!" I cried out, clapping with joy. Water sprayed everywhere, further marking my gown. I raced to wipe the book, but of course it rested dry and unmarred. Again, and again, and again I created water, using the first two handfuls to clean my hands, scouring them with my undergarments, which I am sorry to report never fully recovered from this abuse. The third handful I drank. Doubtless I should have wondered whether magical water might be less than potable, potentially even poisonous. But after hours in that room, dust caked my throat, and however poisonous the water may have been, it tasted sweet as a mountain spring.

Now I noticed the first beams of morning glowing through those delightful gemlike windows. I must depart this room, ere my empty cell be discovered! Hastily I scanned the chamber. Was there anything I had left, any single item or object of importance I should note? But for my footprints and the drops of water surrounding the lectern, the room looked as it had for years untold.

I snuffed the candles and raced down the stairs, now panicked as well that the magic doorway might be sealed. To my heartfelt relief, however, the portal presented the same tangible doorjamb, with only the faintest hint of a filmy barrier. No one had yet arrived; that was one fear eased. I took the last steps two at a time and then, with the overwhelming sensation that my life would never again be the same, I stepped through the veil. Oh, how I now loved this wretched little room! How powerful my gratitude to the queen for imprisoning me within this cell!

Filthy though I was, I threw myself down on the mattress, my mind racing with a great storm of ideas, plans, and notions. I had so, so much to consider.

SEVEN

HALF AN HOUR LATER, deep in dreamless sleep, I found myself being shaken awake in the rudest possible manner.

When Queen Sophia relegated me to this tower cell, she instructed Lady Beatrix to tend to my attire that I be clothed appropriately for classes, dance lessons, riding, meals, and the formal dinners I so abhorred. Utilizing the ever-growing wardrobe in my Peach Rooms, Lady Beatrix would select a seemly ensemble. Yet the lady discovered soon enough that the climb to my cell taxed her greatly. Moreover, I believe she suffered from claustrophobia, so profound was her reaction to that dark and narrow staircase. Thus, with the queen's blessing, she delegated the actual task of dressing me to Hildebert, a formidable handmaid who had little interest in my rank or susceptibility to bribes and was not above the application of brute force. I would emerge from my cell perspiring but dominated, to present myself, should she be available, for Sophia's inspection.

At the moment, however, it took all Hildebert's efforts to awaken me. "What have you done to yourself?" she grunted. "You're covered in filth, you are!"

I blinked, struggling to gather my wits.

"And what are you doing in your gown yet? You never even donned your nightdress!"

"No one undressed me," I answered peevishly but with undeniable truth.

"Milady will have to see this herself!" So saying, Hildebert tossed me aside and stomped away, pausing just long enough to lock me in.

I remained sprawled, laboring to recall the past hours. My hands, swollen and stiff, brought back Sophia's beating. And the tower room . . . had I dreamt it? My gown was irreparably soiled; that was one reassurance. And my curls still reeked with that unmistakable stench of burnt hair.

Leaping off my pallet, I rushed to the wall. In daylight the stones appeared doubly solid, absolutely impregnable. And yet, as I reached out, my hand slipped into them as though into water.

Why did I now suddenly have this power? But, I realized,

I had never touched this particular wall before. No one traipses about a castle fondling every rock and bit of mortar. It was a plain, dull expanse of masonry, the likes of which I'd seen for hours on end every day of my life. Perhaps, indeed, the portal opened for everyone.

Soon as this thought sprang into my head, I heard Hildebert's stomping return. I remained in place, startling her as she opened the door.

"We're going to see her," she announced with a scowl.

"Who?" I demanded, with a petulance that before this day had come automatically to my lips; now I had to force the performance.

"Lady Beatrix, of course it be! I'd take you to the queen, but Her Majesty's suffering from a touch of headache."

That was interesting news, or would be when I had time to dwell on it. At the moment, however, I simply stamped my foot. "I'm not going."

As a red cape enrages a bull, so did this capture Hildebert's attention. "Oh, you're not, are you?" She advanced, arms wide.

As she closed in, I leapt forward and caught her formidable middle. The woman staggered back.

Anticipating that she would fall through the secret portal,

I intended to snatch her away, and distract her through tantrums until the incident slipped her mind. To my surprise and great relief, I was spared this, for her head hit the rock—the very rock into which I had just plunged my hand—with a crack that resounded like a whip snap.

Raging, the woman lunged at me and delivered a great cuff that even at the time I knew I deserved. Our balance of power thus restored, she led me to Lady Beatrix.

❀ ❀ ❀ ❀

Hildebert had had no sensation of the doorway! To be honest, if one were to rank the castle's occupants on their potential for magical powers, Hildebert without question would appear near the bottom of the list. Nonetheless, I now had proof that my abilities were unusual if not unique. Perhaps 'twas my ancestors' blood after all.

As I scurried to match Hildebert's quick pace, footmen stiffened with unusual crispness; maids who had rarely acknowledged my presence now curtsied low. Had I considered the matter, I would have attributed it to my preposterously filthy appearance. Lost in my thoughts, however, I scarce noticed the reception.

Lady Beatrix, when we arrived at her chambers, puffed

in horror. "Princess! What have you done?" Apparently we had interrupted her in the middle of her toilette, for she lacked rouge on one cheek.

I repeated, not having another answer, "No one undressed me."

"And so you ended up like this! Did you roll about on the floor? I cannot believe it."

Neither could I. How would anyone who had seen my sterile cell suppose for one moment that it held dust enough to soil a handkerchief, let alone my voluminous and many-layered gown? But I overestimated the opinion in which I was held. Lady Beatrix apparently believed me slovenly enough to manufacture my own dirt. (The fact that I potentially *could* manufacture dirt was beside the point.) With a dramatic sigh, she released me to my bath.

The combination of hot water, my warm breakfast rolls, and a virtually sleepless night worked as an inexorable soporific. Arriving at the ballroom for my dance lessons, I dropped at once onto a divan.

"Her Highness must stand for the first step," chided plump little Monsieur Grosbouche.

"No," I answered, too exhausted to wheedle. "I won't."

Lady Beatrix examined me. "Very well, then." And she

flounced away, settling with Monsieur Grosbouche on the far side of the ballroom. With a last glare in my direction, the two began to discuss the latest fashions in wigs and how these prizes might best be acquired.

Normally I would have puzzled over this unprecedented liberty. I was far too weary to notice, however, and instead collapsed at once in sleep. When I awoke, the adults were still talking wigs (is there, pray tell, enough substance in the topic to fill a minute, let alone hours?) and the time had come to dress for dinner.

Queen Sophia did not join us. Apparently her headache, or what we may euphemistically term headache, continued to plague her. Lady Beatrix and I ate in silence, I counting the moments until I could return to my cell, and she doubtless still caught up in wig prospecting. I did notice, however, that my helpings were larger than usual, and I smiled gratefully to the footman, who bowed low in response.

As Sophia was not present, Lady Beatrix escorted me to the queen's reception room, where Hildebert met us, my nightclothes over one arm. Traditionally my disrobing and donning of nightdress involved no small amount of sharp words, slaps, and, on one dismal occasion, the toe of a boot. Tonight, however, I tolerated Hildebert's rough handling and sharp tugs with the patience of a mannequin, for the sooner she finished, the sooner my new life recommenced. Several times the handmaid scowled, doubtless wondering to what diabolic act my new docility was leading, but I did not rise even to this ripe bait. Instead I climbed into bed and, as she gathered the last of my dinner garments together, wished the woman good night. With a snort of disbelief, Hildebert marched out of the room, as always locking the door behind her.

No sooner did I hear the faint echo of the staircase door closing far below than I was through the portal. Oh, to think that only twenty-four hours earlier I had not known of this! What a transformation in one's life a day can make.

As I rushed up the narrow staircase, dust already swirling around me, my fingers suddenly brushed cloth. I shrieked aloud as the material collapsed, smothering my short frame. Through fortune alone I maintained my footing, staggering down the steps, ripping and clawing at the enveloping fabric.

My heart pounding, I fled back to my cell. There I discovered myself in possession of a cloak of heavy black wool, complete with sleeves and grosgrain detailing. Impulsively I donned the garment. It fit perfectly, from the deep hood to the snug cuffs to the hem that just brushed my toes. What ideal protection! So swathed, I could spend hours in my dusty secret room and emerge with pristine nightdress, immune to suspicion.

But, I realized, frowning to myself, last night climbing the stairs I had felt naught save stone. And, too, why did the cloak display no frosting of dust? It looked spotless, though discovered in a passageway caked with filth. Perhaps some magical force had placed it there.

I shivered, then chided my cowardice: any force that so provided for me should be considered more ally than adversary. With a firm jaw and only slightly tremulous fingers, wrapped in my new wool armor, I passed again through the wall and up the stairs.

My suspicions of a magical presence increased when I reached the room itself. There lay the spell book, my footprints before it. But the pages had changed! In lieu of the Elemental Spells was an even more disquieting series of images, topped by an immense and unreadable title.

Disappointment coursed through me. The pages, solid as stone, would not turn, hard as I tried; I would gladly have tossed the book out the window, but the volume proved as immovable as its leaves. What good be this spell, whatever it was? Pleased at least to remember the words for elemental

fire, I lit the candelabra that I might … closely. The illustrations made no sen… drops to the ground and perishes, for a … body. Her pursuers gather about the corp… away unnoticed. Later the ghost reappears … would descend a staircase, into the corpse, … turns to life. Inserted between these larger in… grams of hand gestures and phonetic phrasing o…

A body returned to life was black magic; … knew. Perhaps the presence in this wizard room … benevolent after all. Even the heavy Gothic script o… unnerved me. Wondering what path of villainy I mig… now be treading, I sounded the name out, struggling … the foreign pronunciation: "Die Doppelschläferin." Ben… this, I could espy, smaller but in the same heavy text, "T… Sleeping Double."

Ah, the body in the sketches *slept,* not perished. Still, I saw no point to the exercise. Why go to the trouble of such a complicated spell solely to nap?

At this moment, I heard a sound from below that froze my blood: the turn of the lock in my cell's door. I flew for the stairs, but too late; already feet trod the floor below. A girl cried out "Dear heavens, she's gone!" and raced away.

rushed down, tossing my cloak aside as I leapt through
ortal and into bed. Quick as I was, I barely pulled the
kets to my chin before the door crashed open and Queen
hia strode in, a panicked handmaid behind her.

"Your Majesty," I said, attempting to sound both sleepy
d unwinded.

"What is the meaning of this?" snapped the queen. Where were you?"

"In bed, Your Majesty"—this as innocently as I could manage.

Sophia spun on her handmaid. "Is this sport on your part, to toy with us?"

Relieved though I was that the queen had an alternate target, I could not but feel for the girl. She did not deserve punishment for my transgression.

"Your Majesty," I interjected, "I beg your leave. I must inadvertently have hidden myself in the bedclothes. Surely your maid overlooked me in the shadows of this room. So soundly did I sleep that doubtless I did not hear her cry."

The queen glowered, as I had never spoken so solicitously, or so well. Perhaps Lady Beatrix's insipid phrases were making some impact after all.

"I apologize with all my heart, Your Majesty, if I caused even the slightest discomfort."

"We appreciate your humility," the queen said at last, unable to find fault with my penitence, and doubtless swayed by my flattery. "Perhaps your time here serves you well after all."

"I cannot but believe it, my queen. And I promise henceforth always to sleep in a manner that best reveals me to others."

This time I must have gone too far; I could scarce contain a guffaw at my phrasing.

The queen, however, accepted all groveling at face value. She nodded and turned to depart.

My success emboldened me. "Your Majesty, if you please—why did your maid this night come in? Is there some crisis?"

The surprise on the queen's face mingled with another emotion I could not identify. Had she been any other, I would describe it as embarrassment. "No crisis exists. We only . . . we had concern for your comfort."

Ordinarily I would have brushed this off as blatant fabrication. But the distress the answer gave her indicated, hard as this might be to accept, that the woman spoke true.

I settled in my bed as the queen sealed me in once more. The snap of the bolt, I must say, was softer than I had ever heard.

Though I longed to ascend at once to my secret enclave, I lingered, having no desire to be twice caught missing. Why on this of all nights would the queen concern herself with my comfort? Why, I now mused, had Lady Beatrix permitted me to sleep through dance lessons? Why had I received larger portions at dinner, and unprecedented recognition from the castle staff generally, all this day?

My first thought brought my heart to my throat—given the terrors, excitement, and turmoil of the past day, I marveled my heart still beat at all. They knew of my magical powers and sought to appease me!

I quickly rejected this, however. My "powers" were yet so paltry as to be laughable. Lighting candles, producing a mouthful of water . . . these hardly ranked as sorcery. Moreover, I knew the queen; if she had any inkling of my activities, she would have removed me at once from my cell.

The truth, when it arrived, stunned me with its obviousness. So preoccupied was I with my magical ventures that I had forgotten completely, to the point of overlooking even the stiffness in my hands, my battle with Sophia the evening before. Twice she had put all her strength into breaking me, and twice I had withstood her. She, Beatrix, and all their ilk might consider me as dumb as a dumpling, but weak I was not, and clearly they strained to avoid another confrontation.

Thus I learned that with enemies it does not require magic alone to shift the balance of power.

EIGHT

THIS IS NOT TO SAY, mind you, that magic does not provide assistance. If earlier I only suspected a mysterious propitious force aiding my training, I now knew it as incontrovertible fact. The girl in the wizard room's spell had avoided her pursuers by splitting herself in twain, the sleeping portion serving as distraction while the more active half went about her business. I had not pursuers per se, but I suffered myriad prying and suspicious opponents. I had escaped the queen's wrath once; I might not be so fortunate again. I, too, required a sleeping double to remain in the cell while I occupied myself without distraction above. I determined to spend all night, if need be, mastering the Doppelschläferin.

As it emerged, facility—I could not claim mastery—was more the work of three fortnights than one night alone, taking me deep into autumn. The words of the spell proved nigh impossible to memorize, and for the first time I cursed my ineptitude with foreign tongues. Memorization I considered imperative, however, for the spell was initiated in the prone position, and, enthusiastic as I might be, I could not bring myself to recline on that carpet of droppings and dust. Instead I would strain to pack as much as I could into my small brain, hurry down the stairs while I yet retained the information, arrange myself on my humble bed to match the illustrations, and then mutter out gibberish. As the nights progressed, I took to lingering longer and longer on the pallet, ostensibly awaiting results but more often than not dozing. On more than one occasion I returned upstairs to find the book sealed shut, and I confess that my resentment was more than overcome by my relief at now being permitted to sleep. I could not help but notice that in this regard the book, inanimate though it was, cared more for my welfare than any human in the castle.

Eventually I did produce a reasonable Doppelschläferin. My first attempt left me screaming in fright, for the figure I had created lacked arms and legs, and most resembled a dismembered corpse. Lucky I am that my room lay out of earshot of the queen, else this narrative would end now. Upon composing myself I returned to the book and with great effort managed to negate, or rather to complete, the spell, for the objective is only the temporary separation of a body from its double. This experience taught me a powerful lesson, and never again did I attempt a spell without first learning how to undo my work.

A Doppelschläferin, should one not be familiar with this particular magic, is the visual embodiment of its creator. The double remains prone in a sleeplike state and, to the best of my efforts anyway, cannot be woken. Furthermore, as I learned to my great embarrassment, the double retains its maker's clothing. On first completing the spell successfully, I found myself standing as bare and shivering as a newborn child in the middle of my cell. (The illustrations had discreetly overlooked this detail.) With time and much practice, I was able to retain at least a thin camisole and petticoat, quite reassuring to my modest nature, and it caused no end of frustration to Hildebert that I insisted each night on wearing them under my nightdress. Similarly, in order to rejoin my double I had to strip down to this semi-exposed state. One night, exhausted from study, I attempted to step into the Doppelschläferin while still in my heavy cloak, and the cloying, choking sensation it produced in my rejoined body was so nightmarish that I never again failed to undress.

Unfortunately, however long my Doppelschläferin slept,

I never woke from my division rested. Indeed, the remerging of my two bodies produced a confusion of effects I could never predict. I might awaken with spotless hands; at other times they were filthy as ever. At breakfast one morning Lady Beatrix shrieked over a spider in my hair that had doubtless been on me, or rather on the conscious part of me, since midnight. Needless to say, I resented such discrepancies and would strive to make my two selves as similar as possible before recombining, scouring my hands, feet, and face at the conclusion of every magical session.

This task turned out to be much easier than I would have thought. My cell's only furnishing beyond the bed and chamber pot was a stone washbasin built into the wall. The point I had never understood, as the cell contained no tap or cistern, and no servant ever hauled wash water up that staircase. Once I learned the Doppelschläferin with more or less proficiency, however, the book returned to the Elemental Spells, and I set myself anew to this familiar subject. Soon enough I could produce great handfuls of water that quickly filled my basin.

My satisfaction swelled still further with my next discovery: I could produce a small handful of flame even underwater, the surface bubbling and steaming as if I had magicked myself a miniature fumarole. As October, and then November, settled over the castle, sending winter chill into my exposed tower, this trick proved essential, and the production of my own hot wash water gave me more pride than I had known in all my life. Working away with two bits of cloth—one to plug the basin, the larger to scrub away all evidence of the wizard room—I felt as independent as a veritable mountain man.

❖ ❖ ❖ ❖

Doubtless a thoughtful reader might at some point wonder how my days passed between these momentous nocturnal events. What of war, the threat of Drachensbett, my father, and Xavier the Elder? To be sure, war had not yet transpired, though the people of Montagne (myself excepted) yet hummed with preparations as a hive of bees prepares for winter. Drachensbett continued to deny any role in the killings of King Ferdinand and my mother. The king's absurd belief in the presence of dragons atop Ancienne determined even his military strategy, for he appeared willing to sacrifice the immediate capture of Montagne in hopes that our grateful citizenry would at last agree to this fairy tale. Yet even I, the most gullible consumer of fiction in the two nations and perhaps the sole practitioner of actual magic, could not consent to this patent and insulting deceit.

Lord Frederick, our kingdom's esteemed ambassador, had departed Chateau de Montagne in early summer that he might work abroad to avert warfare, though I am ashamed to report I had little concept of the lord's work. Diplomatic correspondence I never saw; its contents were certainly not discussed at dinner. Whether this stemmed from the queen's inherent reticence, her insistence on forever practicing the art of useless conversation, or her suspicion that neither of her companions had the intelligence to manage a dialogue on politics, I could not say. I knew only that war, for whatever reason, had not yet commenced.

My political naiveté was not helped, to be sure, by the fact that my activities during day-lit hours elapsed in a stupor of either napping or yearning to nap. In searching for a technique to manage my chronic exhaustion, I discovered a singularly brilliant tactic: abject passivity. Whereas before I had objected to Sophia and Beatrix's demands, ignored their edicts, and confronted them at every turn, I now gave way as does a cloud of mist, and more luck would they have had building a house of fog than engaging me in conflict. This solution required almost no energy on my part and furthermore, I was delighted to see, drove the two women quite mad.

At dinner the queen would glower at me as I nodded, half asleep, over the aspic.

"We notice you are not speaking, Benevolence."

"No, Your Majesty"—this in a quiet voice, my eyes cast downward.

"Do you not agree that conversation is the foundation of a proper meal?"

"Yes, Your Majesty."

She waited for me to continue as I worked my fork into the gluelike blancmange.

"Have you anything to contribute, Benevolence?"

"No, Your Majesty."

"Perhaps you can inform us what you learned today in your lessons."

"I fear I cannot, Your Majesty."

"Did you learn nothing of substance whatsoever?"

"I cannot recall, Your Majesty."

The color high on her cheeks, the queen would surrender, turning to Beatrix for social intercourse. I noticed the wine flowed ever more freely as these dinners progressed, the queen attempting to drown her frustration with her stupefied niece.

This situation became more problematic upon the return of Lord Frederick in October. Given his rank and post, it was to be expected that the lord would join us at dinner, and his presence at the table enlivened the meal to a degree I did not anticipate, having no experience with a charming and solicitous guest. Lady Beatrix now arrived each night looking quite feverish, an effect not solely attributed to her volumes of rouge. Even Sophia brightened, and sat the lord by her right to converse all the better with him. I was relegated to the queen's left, and Lady Beatrix to Lord Frederick's other side, so at times as I gazed across the table, the poor man had the appearance of a wizened gray flower trapped between two relentless butterflies.

Rarely did I look up, however, for always it seemed that Lord Frederick had his gentle eyes upon me.

"How fare you these days, my princess?" he asked one night. "Do your studies please you?"

"Yes, my lord," I answered.

"Are you sleeping well?"

"Oh, yes, my lord. My room is quite comfortable," I added hastily, for I had no interest now in being removed from my cell.

Lord Frederick pondered my words. "You are certainly not the boisterous child I once knew," he said at last.

Having no response, I simply nodded and returned to my meal.

Lady Beatrix took advantage of the ensuing silence to question Lord Frederick for the sixth time—perhaps he might this time be able to recall—on whether women's sleeves, in the courts he had visited, were flocked or flounced.

This topic held even less interest for me than it did Lord Frederick, and I paid not a whit of attention to his response, returning again to my own thoughts. Reality for me began and ended in the wizard room above my cell.

Elemental fire, as I mentioned earlier, was my first and best skill, and I developed it to the point that I could produce a flame with just one hand, which swelled my head to a ridiculous degree. The earth spell held no interest, as I could not see the point. Yes, I manufactured a fist-size rock, and with struggle crumbled it, but to what end? Far more interesting was elemental air, and the book's promise that I might employ it someday to fly. Working diligently, I mastered it enough to send eddies of dust about the room.

Then, climbing to my wizard room one night, I caught sight of an object I had never before noticed, an article that set me nearly swooning in delight: a broom! (Well might one wonder at my myopia, for the wizard room was not five paces across. Yet this little garret had more hidden crannies and shadowy corners than all the rest of the castle combined, and unseen forces besides.) Delighted, I reached for it, anticipating a thrill of some sort. All that my fingers encountered, however, was the thick grime that clung to the broom as it did to every surface of that chamber.

Now I espied a mop and bucket, several petrified rags draped over the bucket's side. I spun about: the book lay tightly closed. At once I remembered our aphorism that the true cook holds the spoon. Such was the room's power, wielding the spoon as it did, that I could almost sense its bray of laughter: *Ha, Princess!* it seemed to say. *If you want to learn to use that broom, you'd best begin by setting your hand to sweeping!*

And so, with greatest reluctance, I did. I must say that

when Queen Sophia banished me to that barren cell with the intent of instilling humility, she could not have dreamt I would spend my nights scrubbing the floor like a charwoman. Indeed, my opinion of charwomen rose immeasurably as the weeks passed, for cleaning that little room proved no minor feat. My first sweeping so filled the air with dust that I coughed for days, and I soon learned that sweeping has no effect if one does not dust, and that dusting has no effect if one does not wash, and washing has no effect if one does not scrub, and scrubbing, worst of all, has no effect if one's cleaning articles are as filthy as the floor itself.

At times I wondered whether there was space in all the world for the volumes of grit and droppings and bits of lint that this room seemed so intent on releasing. I was forever finding a hidden shelf coated in soot, or a dark cabinet with a skull-shaped lock that leered so unnervingly that I feared to turn my back. Countless buckets of wash water I emptied into my cell's basin, trekking back upstairs each time. But I persevered, if only because I sensed that the book would not reopen until its wizard room gleamed, and I discovered, however worn the maxim that hard work softens the heart, that it did do wonders for my mood.

My weeks of cleaning produced other unanticipated

rewards. One night I set to work dusting the mirror that hung beside the stairs, and then, ever diligent, polished the glass until it gleamed. I studied my reflection in the light of the candles (which, no matter how long the marvelous things burned, never shrank in size). "Mirror, mirror, on the wall, who's the fairest of them all?" I asked with grinning impertinence. Certainly not me. My plump, dust-streaked cheeks shone red from my labors, and cobwebs adorned my tousled hair.

My reflection, of course, stared back. My curiosity grew. What purpose, exactly, did this mirror serve? "Are you enchanted?" I asked the glass. No response came. I shrugged and smiled at my grimy reflection. "You're very dirty."

"Yes, you are," my reflection answered promptly.

Needless to say, this gave me such a fright that in my panic I overturned the bucket. Re-mopping took some time. Finally I returned to the mirror.

"How did you do that?" I demanded.

My reflection mouthed my words dumbly in the manner of reflections everywhere.

"You are very . . . complicated!" I spat out.

"I agree, I am complicated," said my reflection.

I shall not inflict upon my readers the remainder of this

burdensome conversation. After much frustration, not excepting my desire to toss the wretched thing on the floor and jump up and down upon it, I determined that this particular mirror only agreed to the truth. That is to say, if I stated a fact that was true, the mirror would confirm it. And if anyone reading this believes it to be the silliest attribute a magical mirror could possibly have, I shall not labor to convince him otherwise.

When, after Herculean effort, I established this, I could not hold my tongue: "You are so *stupid.*"

My reflection did not react. As I considered it, this was actually a positive sign. After all, I was accusing both the mirror—which obviously was not stupid, for it had magical powers as most mirrors do not—and myself as embodied in my reflection. Imagine if my reflection had agreed that indeed I was stupid; what a blow that would have been. The mirror knew, therefore, that I had some innate intelligence.

My opinion of it warmed. I attempted to think of other truths. "Queen Sophia hates me."

Again, my reflection did not react. This, too, I found noteworthy, for not once had the queen indicated otherwise.

I tried again. "Lady Beatrix wears too much paint upon her face."

My reflection broke into such peals of laughter that she had to wipe tears from her eyes. I needed no further confirmation of that truth.

I returned to my foremost enemy. Perhaps I had not phrased the statement clearly enough. "Queen Sophia does not care for me."

My reflection rolled her eyes. "You require magic to verify *that?*"

I giggled. The magic mirror had wit, it seemed, atop its oblique perspicacity. Perhaps it might be used for matters weightier than facial powder. I could—I could determine, once and for all, the fate of my father!

I spun back toward the glass. "My father is . . ." Is *what* exactly? I wondered. Alive? What if I stated this and the mirror did not answer? Would that mean he was . . . dead? Or that the mirror for some inscrutable reason elected not to respond? Perhaps I should say instead, much as I loathed the words, that my father was dead. But what if the mirror agreed? How dreadful it would be to learn this in such a manner. And—here was the core of the problem—*what would become of me then?* What if I could not keep this secret? Observe how delightfully the queen treated me when she believed my father might yet live. I could not begin to imagine my fate should I be orphaned and truly at her mercy.

I ultimately decided to hold my tongue and settle instead for the comfort of ignorance. Not knowing the truth, I retained hope, and that hope I held like a smooth warm stone against my heart.

NINE

As December passed, I required every grain of that hope, for my circumstances grew ever more oppressive. For reasons I could not begin to fathom, the queen became increasingly preoccupied with what she termed my *carriage,* and which everyone else delicately referred to as my girth. To be blunt, it was substantial. In the weeks following discovery of the wizard room, I had given little attention to food. As winter settled in earnest upon the castle, however, and the icy draughts about my ankles brought back memories of hot soups and steaming meat pies, my thoughts returned to these creature comforts. I missed my parents so acutely that I sobbed, for the hunger in my belly only exacerbated the hunger in my heart. It was not simply food I missed: it was *my mother's* food, her warm kitchen and quick kisses as she bustled about her labors. If my father returned—no, *when* he returned, for I must continue to believe—I vowed that he and I would banquet thrice daily while Sophia survived on dry bread and water. So famished was I, considering this scenario, that even the promise of stale crusts had me licking my lips.

Lady Beatrix harped endlessly about gluttony's effect on my marriage prospects. While the topic had always been a prong in her pitchfork, it now grew into a veritable pike. With every morsel I consumed, I was informed that princes most love slender young ladies. As I was as interested in a prince's love as in sticking my fish fork into my ear, I reacted to this by cleaning my plate ever more thoroughly. Queen Sophia could no longer chide me too bluntly, or beat me, with Lord Frederick at the table, and my portions were not quite so minute as they had once been. Nonetheless, hunger hovered always at my shoulder.

One night, preparing my Doppelschläferin spell, I lay upon my pallet wishing—not for the first time—that instead of water and bits of rock I could produce something of substance. A raspberry torte, say, with a pitcher of fresh cider, or a demitasse of melted chocolate such as my mother had permitted me on special occasions. I was growing weary of my wizard room. The spell book refused to open though I had swept and scrubbed every obscure nook and corner. I had puffed and huffed elemental air up and down the broom and garnered only a fit of sneezing in return. Yet I had naught else to entertain me, and by now my body would not sleep, so accustomed was it to these nocturnal escapades. With a sigh, I stepped out of my Doppelschläferin and through the wall. Donning my black wool cloak, I turned—

To this day I struggle to recall my memories of the roomlet at the base of the wizard room stairs. I had stepped into it countless times: a dozen or more instances each night while learning the Doppelschläferin spell, and at least as many when emptying my wash bucket. Yet I cannot remember, try as I might, ever once paying notice to the wall opposite the staircase. Was it solid? Did moonlight filtering through the portal touch it even once? I cannot say. And yet before my eyes, as clear as if it had been there always, was now a staircase *down.*

I shivered, and reflexively glanced about. But for moonlight and dust, I stood alone.

Clearly I was expected to descend; that much I could deduce. With a deep sigh to steady my nerves, I snapped myself a handful of flame and stepped downward.

Immediately my bare feet met masonry rubble and dust. The stairs had not been used in generations, a suspicion reinforced by the chattering disgust with which the castle mice greeted my presence in their private realm. My light provided scant illumination, and, cautious though I was, I could not refrain from stumbling at the first landing I encountered. Regaining my composure, I crept forward again—and screeched in horror as cold fingers brushed my cheeks!

I batted about blindly, inadvertently quenching my light, as hands touched my hair and cloak. I beat them away, then crouched, ready for further attack. As the minutes passed with no sign of another's presence, I gathered courage enough to snap a small flame. The vision before my eyes set me gaping anew, but this time in awe, for I had entered a nugget of gold. The ceiling glittered. Mounted to walls both before and behind me was a shining Montagne hedgehog. The two other sides of this small chamber—a magical room, surely—each contained a door, almost akin to a closet, or hallway—

I began to giggle in relief, and mortification. To my death I shall be stunned that prior to this moment I had not inferred even half the truth. I was in the queen's ex-room, the passage that connected her privy chambers to the castle's main corridor! No fingers had touched me; 'twas only a magic portal, and the same sensation of cool silk I experienced whenever I passed through the portal in my cell.

Testing this theory, I reached for the nearest wall. My hand slipped through easily. I turned to the opposite wall and was thrilled to witness the same outcome. I chortled aloud as my mind raced to set in place each factor in this marvelous equation. Of course! The castle had not been erected by *giants.* It was rather the work of wizards who built such singularly deep walls so as to maintain secret passageways in the walls' midst. This explained the ex-rooms as well. By bisecting the thick interior walls, the ex-rooms provided innumerable portals between secret passageways and public space. Furthermore (and here I confess that my heart near stopped beating, so delicious this realization), I now at last understood the long-standing tradition of keeping the ex-room doors closed. This privacy would allow a magical person—*such as myself!*—to travel about the castle shielded from human eyes.

The sound of footsteps roused me from my contemplations, and I lunged through the closest portal. Not a moment too soon, for a manservant entered the ex-room with a lantern and a bouquet, as Sophia expected fresh flowers every morn. Methodically he passed through the ex-room into her privy chambers, shutting each door behind him, while I secretly observed, near hugging myself with delight at this most amazing turn of events.

* * * *

Oh, the vistas that opened for me that night. Every major wall in the castle contained a secret passageway, the portals always marked by a hedgehog: gilded on ex-rooms, carved into obscure walls and panels, even woven into tapestries. (In the light of day I would discover a hedgehog scratched on the wall of my cell; I had never before noted it.) Through the veiled openings of these portals I observed corridors, parlors, reception areas, the throne room, the ballroom, the grand and desolate king's apartment, workrooms, armories, and stockrooms. The very soul of caution, I refrained from stepping through a single doorway . . . until I reached the royal larders. Stacked before me, a veritable oasis, rose shelf after laden shelf of food. My heart beat fast; my hands began to shake so that my handful of light trembled, then perished. With a cursory test of the doorway, reassuring myself I could reenter, I leapt into the room.

One might assume, given knowledge of my passions, that I would embark on a complete orgy of consumption. This assumption would be correct. And yet, half mad with desire though I was, I had sense enough to avoid the rarest and most notable items. Frosted cakes perched upon their own shelf, for example, I gave wide berth, as cooks monitor such precious foodstuffs most carefully. Instead I enjoyed the oddest but most delectable feast one could imagine: three apples from a packed bin, fistfuls of dried fruit, a moldy quarter of tart that would not be missed, slabs of smoked ham from a half-finished haunch, a mouthwatering spoonful of tallow—well, two spoonfuls; large spoonfuls—a cupful of sugar, deliciously crunchy, more apples still . . . I soon felt quite ill, but continued to gorge in compensation for my months of imposed restraint. Famine, as they say, makes all food a feast.

Finally I halted, my cloak soiled with grease and jam. Why was it that jam always coated me so? I noticed, horrified, that my footprints covered the floor, first gray from dust, then white as I trod back and forth through a patch of flour I had not even noticed. Frantically I scrubbed away this evidence, grateful for my recent education in housekeeping. A second scare came when I could not locate the hedgehog! But no, I had simply mistaken the scratched outline for a random graffito.

Return proved far more strenuous than I had anticipated.

The passageway, though I continued to remind myself that this was illusion, felt ever narrower and more constricting. My physical discomfort grew to intense nausea as I ascended one narrow staircase after another, for the kitchens of course occupied the castle's basement, and my cell the highest tower.

At one point, passing an opening to the servants' quarters, I near exclaimed in surprise. Shuffling toward me, clear as day in the moonlight that poured through a high window, was none other than my tormentor Hildebert, doubtless on her way to the privy. Ill tempered from queasiness, giving no thought whatsoever to the consequences of this rash act, I impulsively decided to exact revenge for the abuse to which the ogress had for so long subjected me. As she neared the portal, I thrust my head through the veil. How horrifying it must have looked, my face materializing out of the wall before her. Adding to the nightmare, I rolled my eyes in a most ghoulish manner.

I can recall few times in my life when disappointment leveled me as profoundly as it did at that instant. Hildebert glanced at my leering face and continued onward without a pause in her step. I pressed my head out further, but she had passed. Her mutter filled the corridor: "Always knew the ruddy place was haunted."

❀ ❀ ❀ ❀

Once, when I was a child playing beneath an open window, that busybody Frau Lungonaso came upon me, and roughly scolded me that eavesdroppers punish themselves. Had I the wit and knowledge, I would have responded that she better than anyone should know. As it was, I had been so busy tucking my wee worm children into their tiny mud beds that I had not even been aware of the adult conversation occurring inside. Be that as it may, her aphorism would ultimately prove more than true.

I awoke the following morn sated, and my preoccupations carried me through another long, tedious day. No sooner had Hildebert locked me in my cell than I verily leapt from my Doppelschläferin. Securing my snug cloak, I headed downstairs at once, so eager was I to begin exploring, and eating as well, for gluttony like most sins inspires hasty vows but few improvements.

As I descended, the steps shimmered in a pale light, and it took me a moment to realize they were illuminated by yet another portal, this to the queen's reception room. In fact, as I peered in, I found myself looking straight into the face of Sophia herself!

I leapt back, cracking my head. Of course she could not perceive me, but the noise caught her attention.

"Is everything quite right, my queen?" asked a familiar voice. Clutching my throbbing skull, my eyes wet with pain, I leaned forward to observe Lord Frederick resting on a chair. I had not known the two were meeting.

"Of course! We heard only a mouse . . . Are you certain, Frederick?"

"My sources give me no reason to believe otherwise. The possibility of Prince Walter's return no longer restrains them."

My father! My breath caught at his mention. But restrain whom from what?

The queen paced. "Then we have no alternative but to marry."

The queen? My jaw fell open. Who would ever want to marry *her?*

Frederick sighed to himself. "I see no alternative."

"Oh, there is an alternative! Drachensbett's absorption

and destruction of our nation. Perhaps water does in fact flow uphill." *At least water does not flow uphill* is a traditional Montagne expression referring to the fact that Drachensbett cannot attack *up* the waterfall. But the queen now seemed to believe an attack was imminent, however much those fiends smirked their regrets over the Badger Tragedy.

"Yes, Your Majesty," the lord murmured, with seeming—and inexplicable—regret.

She resumed her pacing. "We shall host a great ball, inviting every man of rank within six days' ride."

I listened more intensely than ever I had. The queen could not seriously consider marriage. As regent, she had not even a country to offer as dowry. At least, I thought with a shiver, I hoped not.

Lord Frederick's words brought me back to the present. "I believe the announcement of such an event would delay their attack, knowing they have a chance at the throne through legitimate means."

"If *his* son be the mate we select," sniffed the queen. "Regardless, their presumption serves us well, and so shall we hold them at bay until we identify a spouse for Benevolence."

This time I gasped audibly. How dim I was! It was not the

queen; it was *I* whom they intended to marry off as a brainless brood mare.

The queen stepped closer to the portal. She glared—unknowingly, though this was small comfort at the moment—into my face and ran her hand along the very space through which I peered, my lips pursed to silence any betraying breath.

"Are you quite certain we are alone?" she asked, never taking her eyes from the wall.

"I have taken every precaution, Your Majesty."

Finally the queen turned away as I panted in relief. "As we were saying . . ."

"She is young, Your Majesty."

"Not so young," the queen sniffed. "We have seen girls of ten used to avert crises smaller than this. With a decent ally, our country may yet be preserved."

She continued to speak, but I had heard enough. I stumbled back to my room, all interest in exploration snuffed. I was to be married—joined in union forever with as much thought to my feelings as a cook gives the carrots she drops into a pot. *Every man of rank in six days' ride:* that was the population from which they intended to choose? I had met many of these men through my father. Several, indeed, my mother would scarce allow in our home, and now I was expected to *wed* one of them—possibly even the prince of the nation that forever sought to conquer Montagne!

Eavesdroppers punish themselves indeed. Too despondent even to weep, I huddled under my quilts, wishing more than ever for my father. He alone could save me from a fate verily worse than death into which I was about to be so indifferently plunged.

TEN

In the months that followed, all castle activity centered on the ball. Few other topics crossed the queen's lips, and Lady Beatrix regularly worked herself into such a state over the arrangements, every detail of which she considered her fundamental responsibility, that Hildebert took to keeping smelling salts on her person at all times.

Though I regarded Chateau de Montagne, my secret places notwithstanding, as an adequate model of domestic hygiene, I appeared to be alone in this opinion. The staff, augmented by relatives and a scurrying crew of day laborers, laundered curtains, beat rugs, washed walls, scrubbed floors, and polished windows to such a gleam that one could scarce see through them, so reflective their surface. Even I, a princess and heir to the throne, which I could not help but point out in a rare flaunting of my rank that served me no benefit whatsoever, was drafted into the effort.

"Are the guests truly going to be examining *this?*" I demanded, kneeling inside a chest in an obscure hallway far from the ballroom and guest chambers.

"Just keep to your scrubbing," Hildebert ordered.

Lady Beatrix fluttered past in a cloud of fabric swatches. "Remember, Princess, the ball is in your honor. Perhaps you will catch the eye of an eligible young prince and thus free yourself forever from such drudgery."

There is a chance—a paltry one, I concede—that such a tactic might have appealed to me had I been ignorant of the ball's true purpose. Surely the promise that marriage would relieve me of housework (a promise that every sane woman knows as falsehood) had appeal. As it was, however, I simply glowered and renewed my secret vow to remain unwed.

Now could I understand Queen Sophia's constant harpings on my figure. She cared little about my appearance per se, but she required me presentable to snare herself an ally. She had taken protection of her adopted country to heart and appeared ready to defend it with the zeal of a lioness. It caused her no end of frustration that however minuscule my meals, my waist did not shrink, and my cheeks retained a cherubic plumpness more common to well-fed babies than marriageable royalty. Although the news of my impending betrothal broke my appetite as well as my heart, the former soon returned in force, and every night I applied myself with unprecedented gusto to the castle's larders, pantries, and storerooms. It soon took the efforts of two grunting handmaids and a straining corset to provide any hint that my solid form was in fact female. My strangled discomfort at these constrictions was eased somewhat, however, by my satisfaction at the despair my expansion caused my tormentors.

Novice that I was, I considered myself the model of stealth, and I soon expanded my thievery beyond food. Creeping through the servants' quarters, I pilfered a rough pair of trousers, heavy woolen tunic with jerkin, and thick boots and socks, for my black cloak offered no winter protection to my lower limbs, and not nearly enough to the rest of my body. As my days continued to pass in a fog of exhaustion and catnaps, I paid scant notice to the rumors and minor scandals that forever season the human experience. So it transpired that I, ironically enough, was perhaps the last citizen of Montagne, and certainly the last castle resident, to hear of the malevolent powers that now haunted Chateau de Montagne, forcing guards to tread the battlements in uneasy pairs and quaking maids to sleep with charms grasped in their damp little fists.

My eyes were first opened to this crisis one evening at dinner as I picked genteelly at a meat pie, knowing I would soon sate myself in the larder. Indeed, I would dine better than the queen herself, for while the filling was quite savory, the golden crust bore a close resemblance to shoe leather. I knew the location of the pot that held the filling and could scarcely wait to make it mine.

"Dear Princess," Lord Frederick began, startling me to attention, "I could not help but notice you lingering in the north salon ex-room this afternoon."

My cheeks flushed. Whenever I could travel the castle corridors unescorted—a rare event, and thus doubly cherished—I delighted in pausing in every ex-room to plunge my arms through the hedgehogs.

I stuttered through an explanation. My powers of reasoning—of fibbing, if truth be told—were creaky with disuse.

To my great relief, the queen interjected. "Was she perhaps eating something?" she queried the lord, with a suspicious glower in my direction.

Frederick chuckled. "There is little of sustenance in an ex-room, Your Majesty. Though perhaps she conjured some up, it being a witch room, after all."

My fork clattered from my nerveless hand.

"'Tis one of those trifles of Montagne history—I should not be surprised you do not know it. When the castle was first constructed, the ex-rooms were known as *Hexeraumen,* or witch rooms. One can see easily how 'hex room' would evolve to our own vernacular 'ex-room.' Quite fascinating, really, though of course no one today knows the origin of the term." He swirled his wine contemplatively.

I gulped. The *witch rooms.* Extraordinary.

Lady Beatrix gazed transfixed at the old man beside her. Her heavy powder could not hide her pallor, and her hands gripped the table's edge with white-knuckled force. "*Witches,* you say?" she squeaked.

"How interesting," the queen inserted. "Of course, there are no witches in the castle presently, if there ever were, and we would all be wise to silence any discussion indicating otherwise." This last comment she aimed at her lady in waiting.

Lord Frederick only smiled. "I shall do my best, Your Majesty, though surely the gossip will fade as a more rational explanation is found."

"Explanation for what?" I had heard nothing, and now I burned to know.

Lord Frederick laughed. "'Tis only prattle. I would

attribute it to indolence, but the staff clearly toils with heroic effort. Tell me, dear lady, how go the preparations?" So the wise ambassador parried his way from an awkward corner, in the process drawing Lady Beatrix from her panic to her passion.

I seethed, again left ignorant. Enlightenment came swiftly, however. The next morning, I sat as usual in my breakfast nook, awaiting a meal for which I had no appetite. The pleasant serving maid today nigh quivered in fear.

"Do *you* believe, Princess Ben," she whispered, her eyes darting about, "that spirits fill this castle?"

"I have not seen any," I answered truthfully and, I hope, calmly.

"But lights burn in the Wizard Tower! Directly above your room!"

My hand jerked, spilling hot chocolate. "What is this you say? What tower?"

The girl's eyes grew even wider. "The tallest tower. It's called Wizard Tower—didn't you know that?"

"I am afraid I did not," I answered, buttering my roll with a trembling hand. "And lights burn in it? Doubtless it be only moonlight. You know what tricks moonlight plays."

"Might be. I've seen it myself, and it's hard to tell . . ."

Her reassurance faded. "No one can get to that tower, you know. There's no staircase or nothing—even a ladder won't reach. Do you ever hear anything?" She shivered, uttering these words.

"No, of course not. Besides, if no one can get to it, there couldn't be a light inside."

"But it's *magic,* don't you see? And what about the food missing from the kitchen—the cooks are in a state about it. They say it's a *witch.*"

I stiffened. "I prefer the term *sorceress. Witch* is so common."

At once, a barrier dropped between us.

I had not realized I could sound so much like Sophia. "Yes, Your Highness," the girl replied frostily. She curtsied and withdrew, and would speak no further about the subject, no matter how I probed.

Of course my indiscretions had not gone unnoticed! Now that I had sense enough to listen, I heard whispered conversations everywhere, fantastic tales that spread as mushrooms upon each repeating. That the castle had been built by wizards may well have been a source of pride, but it did naught to assuage present fears. Lady Beatrix and Monsieur Grosbouche muttered horror stories throughout my lessons. As one might imagine, Hildebert stolidly ignored all talk, but she was unique in her skepticism. The queen made pronouncement after pronouncement against such chatter, to little effect, and at times the woman appeared just as anxious as Lady Beatrix herself. Not about witches, mind you, but about loss of control, for rumor is as destabilizing to authority as sorcery, if not more so.

❀ ❀ ❀ ❀

Given the great challenges of my life at the moment—my nightly pilfering, my imminent marriage to some unknown specimen of imbecilic manhood, my endless quest for sleep, and now the risk of exposure as every castle resident sought that mysterious culprit—one would be right to express surprise at my growing passion for flying. Nevertheless, fly I did.

The spell was not easy. (Would any of them be?) True, my long hours practicing elemental air now worked to my benefit, but elemental air made up only one small part of the process. The broom's long solitude had faded its enchantment, which needed to be repeated from scratch. Again the wizard room aided me as cabinets unlocked to reveal desiccated bits of eagle's egg in a cloisonné tinderbox; a jar of powdered bat wings; bottled cloud mist (which looked suspiciously like water, though I did my best not to question). Finally the broom pulsated with the slight tingle I had expected when first touching it.

At last came that fateful night when, trembling with excitement, I brought the broom into my cell; small as it was, it had more space than the wizard room. I chanted the nonsensical words, proud my memory served so well. With great precision, mimicking to the very best of my ability the diagrams in the book, I gestured the prescribed movements and poured elemental air across the broom's surface. I finished the ultimate flourish and dropped my hands to my sides. For a breathless moment, naught happened; then the broom rose into the air and hovered at seat height before me.

I shrieked in euphoria. Unable to contain my enthusiasm, I leapt aboard, grasping the handle so vigorously that the broom shot upward, smacking me against the ceiling with a crack that I was certain could be heard throughout the castle. Dizzy with pain, I fell forward, and the broom hurtled to the floor, depositing me in an ungainly mass of limbs, bruises, and tears. After a not inconsiderable time, I managed to gather my wits and dry my eyes, and noticed with relief that broom was far less damaged than rider.

I spent the rest of the night and several more introducing

myself to this unique transport. The key to navigation, I established, was to focus my sights on my destination. Of course, as I practiced only in my cell, my destinations were always quite close: the window, the door, the portal. I became quite adept at turning, as this constituted the entirety of my flight time. My rough men's clothing now proved even more essential, for I needed to sit astride, and in my nightdress the winter air chilled my exposed legs.

Oh, how I longed to soar through the sky! Past the stars, across the moon, over sleeping Montagne and its flag-adorned turrets. Even as I dreamt of this rapture, my wiser side spoke against it. Rumors of witchcraft now burned across the country. Sheep on Ancienne had gone astray; a shepherd boy had not been seen in weeks; spirits with cloven feet tracked ash across the ballroom floor. As far as the truth went, I had seen the ballroom myself, and the prints (well should I know) were only mice. Sheep had been disappearing from the mountain since time immemorial; rational men in rational times agreed the creatures must be tumbling into an unmarked ravine. As for the shepherd boy, I had no insights beyond the knowledge that I was in no way responsible.

Yet tempers were raw, and the castle's populace, tense over the impending ball and doubtless sensing in some intangible way the threat from Drachensbett, promised violence against anyone suspected of sorcery. Better to dart about my cell like a beetle trapped in a jar, and to enter the pantries only when my howling belly could bear hunger no more.

❀ ❀ ❀ ❀

As the festivities drew closer, my days grew ever more oppressive. The ball had emerged as the social event of the winter. Overtaxed though Lady Beatrix might be, it was clear she took the greatest delight in her responsibilities, and were she to perish on the dance floor as the orchestra played its last notes, she would certainly consider her life more than complete.

I, on the other hand, felt precisely the opposite. I spent hours perched like a straw target while dressmakers pinned up fabrics and bemoaned my stature, Sophia snapping that I should stand straighter, as though posture alone caused my apple-shaped silhouette. All subterfuge surrounding the event had disappeared. My mate would be chosen whether I wished it or no; any small effect I might have on the decision would be determined solely by my abilities to charm the man I favored. Sophia spelled this out in grim detail, and it is a testament to her faith in tradition that she, despite all evidence to the contrary and three-quarters of a year in my company, yet believed me capable of such wiles. Better I would have been at pulling parsnips out of my nose than charming any man, even if I so desired it, even if I quadrupled my studies in her unique curriculum.

However, as the saying goes, a clever chicken can escape the crock. I had my wits, my magic, such as it was, and, perhaps my greatest asset, my current reputation. If necessary, I would sleep through the event. More than once in my earshot the queen herself expressed fear of this outcome. Or, heeding the ceaseless warnings that rained upon me, I might simply play the glutton. If my greed had half the effect on the guests that Beatrix predicted, my task would be an easy one.

Kind Lord Frederick, employing the same remarkable intuition that had served him so many decades in service of the Montagne court, must have sensed my scheming, for one afternoon I found myself under his thoughtful eye as I struggled across the ballroom with Monsieur Grosbouche.

"How wonderfully you dance together," he said, choosing the high road of flattery over the boulevard of truth. "If Her Highness so consents, I should be delighted to escort her in the next movement."

I blinked, for rarely did I encounter formality put to such gratifying effect. Regaining my composure, I agreed to his request as Monsieur Grosbouche waddled to the nearest chair, grateful to retie his laces and free himself momentarily from his obstreperous student.

Never had I danced with a partner about whom I felt such consideration, and this unprecedented circumstance required all my concentration. Lord Frederick was a most thoughtful dance partner, and he refrained from grunting the time into my ear. The experience was so altogether foreign as to constitute another activity entirely. It was, dare I say, pleasant.

"My dear Princess," Lord Frederick began.

I stepped on his toes, then apologized most profusely.

"Do not give it another thought. A dancer should be so enthralled with his partner that he pays no notice to such trivialities."

To my great embarrassment, I blushed. That I might be a partner who enthralled had never before suggested itself.

Lord Frederick beamed. "What a joy it is to see you looking girlish. You pass so much of the day somber."

"The ball is quite demanding of us all."

"Ah, yes, the ball . . . it seems the most trivial of undertakings, does it not?"

I nodded, grateful for the opportunity to express myself.

"And yet the fate of our kingdom may very well hinge on it. Did you not know that?"

"The queen implied so—she seems to care a great deal about it . . ."

"Indeed she does. She cares a great deal about *you,* Ben."

This statement caught me so off-guard that I nearly sent us sprawling. "She doesn't in the least!"

"She most certainly does. Remember, she has no experience with children."

"I am not a child!"

"Of course you are not . . . But she, like you, is making the best effort she can."

I scowled. I did not appreciate the notion that she was making an effort. Nor did I want to dwell on whether I was.

"I speak to you as an equal, Ben. Nations larger than ours desire to claim us. If we are to survive, we must build alliances."

"I don't want to marry!"

"Nor do I wish it, not in circumstances such as these. But, odd as it must doubtless seem, a ball is as critical a display of strength as a marching army. Surely you desire to demonstrate our strength to the world?"

I nodded. I did want to display Montagne's strength; I was patriot enough for this.

"Your father would be quite proud of his little soldier. You are a soldier now; I hope you recognize that."

"Yes, my lord," I whispered. I would endure the upcoming festivities, however awful they proved, for my father, wherever he might be. What followed afterward I would confront in the passage of time.

❀ ❀ ❀ ❀

The ball was the stuff of nightmares. Preparations reached a last fevered note; as the guests began arriving the day before the ball, Lady Beatrix outdid herself arranging them throughout the castle in a most politic fashion, with fires in every room against the March chill. A small banquet had been prepared for the early comers, for which I had the most elaborate assemblage of clothing. Interpreting my vow to Lord Frederick to denote the dance itself, I refused to attend, and had such a case of hysterics—false at first, but building to real emotion—that I was excused. Sophia could not have been more disgusted.

The day of the ball was spent preparing me much as one prepares a goose for Christmas, with the same ultimate effect. I was squeezed into my dress despite my ceaseless complaints that I could not breathe; powdered and scented almost to death; painted and primped and polished. My scalp was wrenched near to bits in an effort to squeeze my hair beneath the wig ordered especially for this event. Alas, no matter how the hairdressers struggled, they could not cram it into the hairpiece. Hildebert, boiling with frustration, at last took matters into her own hands and without so much as a word of warning snatched up a pair of shears and lopped off a great handful of my locks.

I was aghast; I would have burst into sobs had not the look on her face warned me off, and so instead I was forced to watch in the mirror, whimpering in misery, as she trimmed my hair short.

"All the ladies do it," she explained, jamming the wig onto my head. Having never witnessed Lady Beatrix wigless, I would not know, but tears ran down my sorry cheeks at this pointless and vicious indignity.

At last dusk fell. The orchestra started its first song, the notes flowing through the castle to fill me with dread. I stood glowering at my wigged and corseted, gloved and painted reflection, my feet already aching in dance slippers more akin to pincers than shoes. "I look ridiculous," I stated, and it did not require a magic mirror to confirm that I spoke the truth.

I remember most how crowded the ballroom appeared compared to its empty vastness most days, and how everyone, man and woman alike, glittered in a polychrome sea of silks, jewels, and powder. I was of course expected to make a grand entrance at the top of the stairs; we had practiced this extensively, and I consider it my lone small victory that I did not end up in a heap on the bottom step. Instead the kings and queens, lords and ladies, princes and princesses, earls, dukes, knights, marquises, and other titles I scarcely knew hovered about to be presented, one by one. I could not recall their names if I tried.

That is not exactly true. I do recall Sophia herself introducing me to the Baron Edwig of Farina, for the hand he offered was, to my surprise, even clammier than that of Monsieur Grosbouche. The man's face was painted almost as thickly as Lady Beatrix's, and he clutched me as though I were a prize he would not quickly release.

"The baron," the queen said, "has traveled five days to attend this fete. He is most interested in making your acquaintance."

"I had heard tales of your loveliness," Edwig simpered, "but none does it justice. Perhaps someday you will match the beautiful queen regent herself."

I glowered at the man, wondering if he had any notion of how ridiculous he sounded. "I trust you are enjoying your stay in our castle?" I asked at last.

"Would that I were, Your Highness. But I am afraid my sleep last night was quite troubled. This morning I identified the source of my bruises"—here he reached into a pocket of his waistcoat—"as a pea that had been tucked beneath my mattress." With a sad smile, he displayed the offending object.

I uttered the first thought that entered my head: "Well, aren't you frightfully rude."

Sophia gripped my arm. "Princess, we must demonstrate our natural sympathy . . . How delicate you must be, Baron, to suffer such discomforts."

"Delicate?" I exclaimed. "He comes into our home and tells us that our beds are full of beans—"

With a bow to the baron, she snatched me away. "He would be an excellent match for us," she hissed in my ear, her fingernails four stilettos in my arm, "and his family produces swarms of offspring."

"But surely you were affronted—"

"Queens neither proffer nor receive insults! If you cannot control your tongue, we demand that you hold it silent."

Oh, how I burned! The very concept that the queen did not proffer insults—the woman could flay a man with more expertise than a cook skins a rabbit. And for her to reiterate, lest for a moment it slipped my mind, that the entire point of this exercise was to mate me to a fecund, well-heeled fop . . . my patience left me entirely.

Fingernails still buried in the flesh of my arm, the queen led us to our next guests. "King Renaldo, Prince Florian, how delighted we are to meet you again. May I present Princess Benevolence."

I curtsied as I had been taught; they bowed. *King Renaldo?* I knew that name; my father had uttered it, many times . . .

"Your brilliance outshines the lights, Your Majesty," the man stated, beaming at the queen.

I remembered now: he was king of Drachensbett! This very man standing before us had ordered the murder of my mother, and Sophia's spouse!

Yet the queen, who better than anyone knew this truth, demonstrated not a sliver of disdain. "It is our greatest delight that you have consented to attend our humble affair this evening."

"Indeed," the king replied—his tone lacking, I was stunned to observe, all guilt, cunning, or malevolence—"knowing of your presence here, I could not have allowed myself to be elsewhere."

His son, I was pleased to note, rolled his eyes at this insipidness. Florian was unmistakably handsome, even to my inexperienced eye, although his sneer negated his good looks. But then, what else could one expect of that country? He scanned the ballroom. "Such an attractive space," he murmured to his father. "So perfectly proportioned."

"You are but one of many men present plotting its acquisition this evening." These spirited words flew from my lips of their own accord.

Prince Florian for the first time paid me notice, his dark eyes squinting in disdain. I did my utmost to match his frigid scowl, though I could not completely suppress a strangled gasp as Sophia's nails sank further yet into my arm. 'Twas some manner of miracle that four pools of blood were not already collecting on the ballroom floor.

Without warning this delightful interchange was interrupted by the return of Baron Edwig. He bowed to our foursome, his wig nearly brushing the floor. "So honored I would be if the fair princess would accept my hand for this dance." For permission he looked not at me—I was only commodity, not a living being—but at Prince Florian, who bowed in return with an expression of exquisite boredom.

So I found myself on the dance floor, all eyes on my performance, as the baron droned away. My only joy came from my discovery, curtsying to my partner at the commencement of our pas de deux, that his slippers featured the exact bows as those of Monsieur Grosbouche. I forced a smile, and within fifteen steps expertly released his laces. Too proud or dim to stop, the baron continued dancing with an ever more shuffling, mincing pace.

So intent was I on this entertainment that I paid his words no heed. "I beg your pardon," I said finally. "The music has quite captivated me."

"Oh, 'tis nothing," the baron warbled, struggling to remain upright. "I was wondering only what think you of Drachensbett."

I could not restrain my tongue. "As a nation, you mean? Or an invading force?"

My candor, combined with his failing footwear, left the baron stumbling. "That is not—what I meant—but how—

oh, behold, the tune has ended . . ." With a bow, he shuffled off, not even feigning an interest in properly concluding our conversation.

Joviality had scarce filled my soul prior to this dance, but nonetheless I allowed myself a healthy dose of indignation at the baron's profound faux pas. How dare that idiot raise the topic of our nations' enmity—with King Renaldo himself not twenty paces away!

My ire must have shadowed my face, for several plucky young men withdrew at my scowling visage. Absently I worked my way along the groaning banquet table, gorging on the delicacies. My gown felt ever tighter, the noise and heat of the room set my ears to ringing, and I was overcome with the yearning to escape this useless commotion and miserable garment. But the grand gilt doors atop the stairs stood in plain view; Queen Sophia, chatting with several of her countrymen, would intercept me in an instant.

There were, however, other options . . .

Behind the table, two prominent pilasters flanked the Montagne coat of arms—including an enameled hedgehog. I glanced about. I was unobserved; apparently I wearied even the most prying guests. In an instant I was in the shadows and through the wall.

The climb had never been more torturous, for I truly could not breathe in my corset. Finally I burst into my cell. Oh, how inviting it looked, how refreshing and simple after the frippery below! I dropped atop my quilt. The spell and gestures required but an instant, and at last I stood gulping down great quantities of air as a Doppelschläferin lay at my feet, still trapped in that horrible gown. Now I could think.

In this first moment of clarity, I realized I could tolerate this existence not a moment longer. Not the wardrobe, not the interminable and useless instruction, not the discussions of invasion and matrimony, for both of which I was absolutely unsuited. If the castle believed my only contribution to the preservation of Montagne was my unwilling and unsolicited presence at the altar beside a man I would abhor, then the kingdom was as good as lost. My Doppelschläferin could better serve that role, so uninterested was anyone in my intelligence or opinion.

I stared down at my sleeping double. If *that* was what the nation wanted, then that is what it would receive. I had fulfilled my promise to Lord Frederick. My life henceforth would be my own. I could fly a broom with middling skill; I knew how to clean. I would find some distant land where I could work an honest job in return for three meals a day.

With time, when I was very old and in my twenties, I might find a man to love, not one forced upon me . . .

With swift decisiveness I pulled on my warm wool clothes and cloak. Snatching up my broom, its magic pulsing through my hand, I strode to the window.

No sooner had I touched the latch, however, than I heard the most horrifying sound of pounding footsteps.

In a panic, I fumbled to open the window.

Outside my door, a man cried out, "Your Majesty—she could not be here—"

"I must find her!" Sophia cried wrathfully. The key turned with a blood-chilling snap, the door slammed open, and she burst into the room, fury contorting her face.

I froze in terror.

"There you are!" she roared—not at me, but at my poor, lifeless Doppelschläferin! Nonetheless I reflexively pressed myself against the glass.

My movement caught her eye. "Touch not that girl, fiend!" she shrieked.

I gaped back at her. She did not recognize me! My hooded cloak, a room drenched in shadow—

"Seize the witch!" she commanded the two guards behind her.

Grimly intent, the guards stepped toward me, their arms spread wide. I would be seized, interrogated, even burnt—

Blindly I groped behind me—the latch released at last! I pushed the window open with all my strength.

The guards lurched closer as Sophia shrieked instructions.

I took a deep breath, redoubling my grip on the broom.

The guards' massive hands lunged for me, for one terrifying moment grasping my cloak. At that instant I dove out, plunging through the night to my doom.

Part Three

In which my newly acquired talents prove to be of little benefit in a harsh and unfamiliar territory

ELEVEN

CHATEAU DE MONTAGNE STANDS atop a precipice, the castle's northern façade rising straight from the living rock. From the Wizard Tower, the highest point of the castle, to the cliff's base far below is a vast distance, absolutely vertical and terrifying to behold. Such was the void through which I now hurtled, scrabbling at the air itself as I clutched my useless broom. Wind roared past my ears, my cloak billowed like a living beast. My life would end in a matter of heartbeats.

Forlornly I forced my eyes open to see the world one last time. I was hurtling headfirst to the ground—I could spy the lights of the castle between the toes of my boots—

And then, I slowed. *The lights of the castle!* I pulled the broom closer, clinging to it like a vine, never taking my sight from that focal point. How close I came to the ground I will never know, but I can aver that the castle was far, far above as I began my struggling ascent.

To my shock, the castle, as I neared it, burst into flame. Or so it appeared, for massive bonfires sprang to life atop every watchtower, and pealing alarums urged soldiers to their battle stations. Was this the Drachensbett attack, at this moment? A great shout broke out—an arrow hissed past my head. More arrows followed, and in my panic I lost all concentration and plunged anew through the air, thus providentially escaping those deadly missiles.

Should one ever be in a position to learn the art of flying a broom, I strongly advise against this particular scenario, above all if the sum of one's sole previous experience has consisted of circumnavigating a narrow tower cell in a manner most resembling a carnival ride. How I survived these first minutes I do not know, and I can only assume that the same abstruse yet benignant forces directing my magical education preserved me now from death.

Soldiers continued to launch volleys in my direction, including flaming arrows of terrifying dimension. Powerful searchlights probed the sky, seeking me out. My great-grandfather had found lighthouses endlessly fascinating and designed a martial equivalent to ferret out nocturnal invaders. Though I had always gloated over my forebear's ingenuity, I now cursed his cleverness. As I could barely steer, I had no notion how to avoid these bedazzling rays, and indeed at one point found myself blinded, trapped like a fly in a web. Panicking anew, I again lost all control, and in my tumbling evaded the beams.

Desperately I scanned the blackness around me. Surely there was another target, something in that pitch of night I might use as beacon to escape.

As if answering my unspoken plea, the moon drifted into sight through a litter of clouds. At once I shot toward this crescent. Faster and faster I climbed, fear driving me to ever greater speeds. And then, to my horror, the moon slipped away, quick as it had emerged. I must not fail! I kept my eyes on that one spot, convincing myself I could yet see it. Miraculously, I continued to rise.

Still, searchlights probed the sky. Much as I raced, they swept faster toward me. I was snared! A second joined, a third. Try as I might, I could not evade these spotlights. A missile, large as a catapult stone—perhaps, indeed, that it was—hurtled past. If struck, I would perish in an instant . . .

I plunged into the cloud itself. At once, icy fog swallowed the damnable searchlights. Relief was followed instantly by panic. I could barely tell up from down, and had no notion of the direction in which I should fly. Yet on I flew, remaining on my broomstick through grit alone, knowing I must not return to the valley below and the soldiers who longed to blast me from the sky.

The air grew colder, if that was possible, and I adjusted my clothing as best I could against the chill. Weariness flooded my bones, and I could not but wonder what strength my effort was costing, and how much longer I could survive.

Suddenly my foot brushed an object! Almost plunging from my broom in astonishment, I peered down and could just distinguish snow-covered treetops below me. I must be on the mountain itself: perhaps near abreast the summit! Now would be the ideal time to cross Ancienne, find some obscure hamlet that knew nothing of Montagne or Drachensbett or witchcraft, and there settle into a new life.

Steeling my heart, I set myself to the daunting challenge. A challenge it was, too, for the air itself shriveled and weakened at this height. Closer I dropped to the mountainside, for I now needed it as guide. How carefully did I pick my way! My eyes ached from strain, and my back from my crouched position.

Without warning a mammoth boulder, scabbed with ice, loomed before me out of the darkness. I turned, but too late—I lost all control. I crashed into the stone face, a tangle of limbs and cloth, and, falling to the mountainside, knew no more.

❀ ❀ ❀ ❀

My violent shivering roused me as rose tints painted the eastern sky. Much labor it required to recollect each tumultuous event of my recent past, how I came to occupy this patch of snow. My head throbbed, and my fingers, though numb with cold, located a lump half the size of an egg on my forehead. Packing more snow still against my skull, I sat up and attempted to take my bearings.

My precious broom lay not two paces away, shattered in a half-dozen fragments. I crawled over, silently praying, but could tell with one touch that all hope was gone. No hint of magic tingled through the splinters of wood, which now looked no better than kindling. It, and I, rested on a bank of snow. Above me, an ice-coated cliff rose seemingly without break to the heavens. Escape, should I manage it, wherever my ultimate goal (and one can be sure my enthusiasm burned much dimmer in the light of dawn), would only be down.

The snow alone proved a formidable obstacle. At times I

found myself waist-deep, forcing each leg forward with all my strength. Never did the powder rise to less than my knees, and more than once I plunged suddenly into a drift over my head—most entertaining had I been a child within sight of my warm home and a bubbling kettle of chocolate, but not in the current circumstances. Neither can I omit mention of the boulders that turned my path into a rugged obstacle course, or the wind that sent blinding fistfuls of snow into my eyes and ears, and down my collar.

My situation only grew worse. Stumbling, I nearly tumbled off yet another cliff obstructing my route. Panting with fright, I began to climb down hand over hand, feet scrabbling for position. My hot perspiration chilled to ice; my fingers numbed. Falling the last bit, I touched ground again, relieved past measure though the impact knocked the wind from my body.

My hands ached with cold, and at last I could manufacture a small flame while I collected my breath and thoughts. As I gazed back up at that stony face, I could not but marvel at my accomplishment. Desperation, it would seem, makes heroes of us all.

Now I noticed, too, peculiar markings on the stone. At

one point a fissure broke the cliff's face rather as a door breaks a wall, and aside this opening were several scratches —fresh, to my eyes at least—that appeared, improbably enough, to be letters. With one finger, careful to maintain the flame in my other hand, I traced them. They *were* letters! They had to be, so precisely had they been scratched into the lichen and rock:

H R H W K M

I frowned. "HRH" I knew, as it is forever in use in official correspondence, an abbreviation for His Royal Highness, or Her Royal Highness as the case might be. But I could make no sense of the final three letters.

At this moment the sun burst fully to life through the eastern clouds. Golden rays bounced off the snow in an explosion of light. Light illuminated the cliff face as well, pouring into the fissure with such intensity that the cleft itself seemed to glow.

The fissure, I could now see, was wide enough to enter. In fact, it opened into a small cavern within the cliff itself. Cold, exhausted, and frightened I might be, but my curiosity remained fresh. I eased my way inside. As I did so, the luminous rays of morning touched the cavern walls, turning the hoarfrost that coated them into a glittering expanse of diamonds. The brilliance dazzled me; so perfectly illuminated, the crystals rendered this frozen space more magnificent than an emperor's palace.

Entranced, I continued forward. The sunbeams slipped down the wall, catching ever more of those frozen gems, and—

There he lay. So entranced had I been by the cave's icy beauty that for a time I did not notice the man on the floor. He, too, glittered as if made of a million gems, for he was encased in a veritable shroud of frost.

Registering at last, I cried out in horror, too frightened to move. It was not . . . it could not be . . . yet I must be sure. I stole forward. The man was of good size; his armor, anyway. His face, however, had shrunk almost to the bone, and its desiccated, cadaverous appearance terrified me. His hands likewise were more skeleton than flesh. Yet the thin prince's crown on his head—worn only for the most formal occasions, I well remembered—glowed gold through the ice, and the Montagne hedgehog showed clearly on his surcoat.

I had found my father. Small wonder no one had discovered his remains, for no team could have searched this far.

No man, I believed—or had believed up to this moment—ever ascended so high up Ancienne.

My father's right hand clenched a dagger, its purpose apparent from the rough scratchings on the wall by his side. Frost obscured many of the letters, and I promptly melted this by breath and flame. Each letter, I well imagined, had cost him dearly as he battled cold and death.

Through the glimmering light I could discern, scraped on the stone itself, the condemning phrase I PURSUED DRACHENSBETT. The next sentence—the final one, the last he ever wrote—brought tears to my eyes, and kneeling at his side, I wept openly. With the last embers of his strength, he had chosen three simple, unforgettable words: FAREWELL, SWEET BEN.

❀ ❀ ❀ ❀

For many hours I sat, ignorant of cold, as the sun moving through the heavens returned this glittering cavern to a dark and frigid tomb. I now understood the letters scratched on the cliff face as my father's initials: *His Royal Highness, Walter, King of Montagne.* Never would my father have referred to himself so formally; such pomp was reserved for Montagne's leader. As he carved those letters, therefore, my father must have known that his brother Ferdinand had already perished and that he was now king. Neither had he bade farewell to his beloved wife; she, too, he knew, was no longer of this world.

Now I had incontrovertible evidence of Drachensbett's role in her death. The shameful Drachensbett king, with his sniveling ambitions, his lying and greed and his sneering son, must pay for the pain he had wrought. Kneeling at my father's side, I vowed revenge. "Farewell, sweet Father," I then whispered in his ear, returning his words. I managed even a formal curtsy, backing from the cave as one does in the presence of a king.

Xavier the Elder, the esteemed soldier who had disappeared with my father that day, I now knew must also rest somewhere on the mountain, dead of wounds or exposure. Surely this information would provide his son some consolation. I would return to Montagne to share this news somehow and rally its people against our despicable foe.

I set off at once. The hour I could not tell, for winter clouds now blocked the sun. My sense of direction, already weak, suffered in the uneven terrain as my hunger grew. I was descending, that much was clear, but however hard I peered about for some indication of civilization—a shepherd, a woolly Montagne sheep, even the hint of a cleared meadow—I discovered naught but the cheeky little birds that continually warned the forest of my presence.

The wind intensified, howling in a most unnerving fashion. Oh, I would never escape Ancienne! How bitter the irony! Now, when at last I had a true goal, one worthy of my parents and station, my dream would be denied me.

Overcome, I collapsed against a tree as the wind, sounding almost like a human voice, shouted past my head. A hiss—and without warning an arrow pierced my arm. I gaped at my limb pinned to the tree trunk. I felt no pain, only bafflement at this inexplicable turn of events. Then, overcome with the shock of the last twenty-four hours, the traumas that piled ever deeper upon me, I fainted.

I came to consciousness in a small copse of trees. Dazedly I struggled to open my eyes, then was shocked awake by the stabbing agony of my arm. What I saw sent me reeling: an arrow pierced the sleeve of my woolen tunic, now saturated with blood, and my swollen, violet-colored wrist. One tentative movement produced such a wave of pain that I knew at once my forearm was broken.

Despairing at this awful image, I noted for the first time

deep voices. Peering about, I realized with a start that I was not sprawled amid tree trunks but rather in a half-circle of men.

"He knows of our presence," said one, fingering a broken arrowhead—doubtless the remainder of the projectile now embedded in me.

They thought I was a boy? Both ears pricked, I listened further.

"Thanks to you!" snarled a second man. "He had no sense of us otherwise." He prodded me with his foot. "Whence hail you?"

Numb though I was with pain and cold, I knew well enough that informing them I was the better half of a Montagne witch-princess would not bode well. My teeth chattering, and not only with chill, I answered: "The mountain, sir."

The man sighed. "We know that. Which side? Drachensbett or the other?"

"The—other, sir. Montagne."

The men eyed each other. "Must be that missing shepherd boy," one offered.

"That lad's been lost for months. This one"—again a boot met my flesh, harder this time—"is far from starvation." They chuckled.

"Perhaps it's enchantment," said another, "being Montagne . . ."

"Ha! An enchanted boy wouldn't bleed and whimper so." Again they laughed.

"We must dispose of him. He can't return knowing of us."

The second man—he appeared to be their leader—spoke again. "Better would it be to slaughter some fat piglet than this creature; that at least we could eat. This boy's death would only bring trouble upon us." For a third time I was kicked. "What be your name, piglet-boy?" he asked.

"Um, B-Ben."

"Well, Piglet Ben, you belong to us now. Get up."

"Belong—to—whom?" I struggled to my feet as best I could, my eyes streaming from pain.

The man barked a short laugh. "To the army of the kingdom of Drachensbett."

TWELVE

NOT A DAY EARLIER, I aspired to flee my onerous burdens of nobility for a position of anonymous and humble service in another land. Now, to my enormous heartbreak, I had attained my exact wish. Rest assured that the irony of this situation, bitter though I found it, did not escape me.

The patrol that had discovered and accidentally shot me now dragged me back to their camp. That is to say that they cuffed, kicked, and pushed me along, keeping me always to the forefront to prevent my escape, assuming as they did that I knew the route back to Montagne. After some time, the leader—Captain, his men called him—threw one end of my cloak over my shoulder, ordering me to hold the edge with my good hand as a sling for my throbbing arm. His goal was expedience, not compassion, for my moaning pace delayed them. From the snatches of banter I could make out, they had no interest in experiencing the mountain in darkness.

At last, dusk settling around us, we arrived at a double row of huts built of fresh-hewn logs. Returning scouts greeted my captors boisterously as we approached, paying me no more than a second's notice.

The captain ordered me brought to the mess hall, for the camp's cook was also its surgeon. One look at the man's hands and I wanted no taste of either of his professions, but no other option was presented, and in a moment's time I found myself laid out on a table, the cook's grimy fingers prodding my wound. Without warning he jerked the arrow's remains from my arm, and again I fainted. When I came to, the broken bone was already set, and my arm splinted.

Glad as I was that the rags securing this splint were at least clean, I wished he had taken the time to soak them in aqua vitae, for my mother always swore of the healing powers of strong spirits. I knew better than to request this, however, for already I sensed the man had no interest in instruction, least of all from a whimpering young prisoner.

Without a word, the cook plunked an earthen bowl of stew at my side and returned to his stove. How good the stew tasted in reality I cannot say, but at that moment, drunk with hunger and pain, I considered that hodgepodge of beans and old meat the nectar of the gods, and I polished it off promptly.

"Huh," grunted the cook as I brought my empty bowl to him—ostensibly returning it, but in truth hoping for a second serving—"you eat well enough. But you cry like a girl."

I started. Of course I did! But, no, they could not learn that. Whatever fate might befall a female prisoner, I did not want to discover it. Instead I nodded in what I hoped was a masculine fashion.

"Start scrubbing those," he directed, jerking his head at a mountain of soiled pots and bowls.

"But—" This in the deepest voice I could manage.

"Don't 'but' me," he snarled. "Prisoners work for food, and they thank me for it, too."

So I did, and set to work on the pots, my belly still growling.

Here I made the most awful discovery: my broken arm, in addition to aching with throbbing intensity, had been wrapped so thoroughly that I could not wiggle any part of my right hand. My injury and its dressing meant that I *could not move my fingers.* Washing dishes was thus problematic at best. Far more horrifying, however, was the realization that the spells over which I had labored for so many months were now as good as useless.

In the days that followed, it became clear that I was without doubt the most worthless human being these Drachensbett men had ever met. I could not chop wood or clear dinner bowls; my skills as bootblack were nonexistent; I failed even at tugging arrows from a target the soldiers had erected.

But, I counseled myself, at least no one discerned my sex. Filthy, my hair close-cropped, I spent my days, and nights as well, in a bundle of fabrics that would have disguised the most feminine of silhouettes, and my silhouette was far from feminine. Even without my cloak, I sported a tunic covered with a heavy wool jerkin, these topped with a shapeless and bulky knitted jersey, more suitable for fisherman than soldier, that I had unearthed my first day in the camp. In fact, its past life on the sea was apparent from its stench, but I quickly learned to sacrifice delicacy for warmth.

Anonymity, however, was derived less from appearance than from station. My past ten months in the castle had exposed me to a ceaseless outpouring of attention. Much as I disliked it, I had grown accustomed to constant observance by servants, teachers, guests, and residents of Montagne, little though I came in contact with this last population. In the Drachensbett camp, however, I learned the truth that men forever look upward. The cares, needs, clothing, demeanor, and indeed gender of those of inferior status bear them little concern. Most days I spent with tears dried to my cheeks, having no water, looking glass, or incentive to wash them, and even these did not attract attention. As prisoner, I was considered drudge for whoever claimed me first, and that claim was accompanied by only the most perfunctory of glances.

The cook quickly took me as kitchen slave, even chaining me to his great empty cooking pot each night so that I would not escape. Stirring meals, scrubbing dishes as best I could one-handed, serving up great steaming globs of food—such became the cycle of my days, and though the pain in my arm gradually faded as the bones reknitted, the pain in my heart only grew.

It was, however, in working for the cook that I discovered my one ability. Self-defense, evasion, navigation—all these I desperately required, and had not. Yet I could still, one-handed, light fires. No matter how wet the wood, how sparse the kindling, how drafty the hearth, in the space of minutes I produced a working flame.

My labors soon included warming the officers' quarters before they arose each morning. (The soldiers, as soldiers everywhere, were expected to suffer.) The first day of this assignment, the captain watched my labors from his bed, though I hid my hand gestures as best I could. "That's quite a talent, Piglet," he said, using the designation by which I was universally known, to my enormous shame, in the camp. "We'll have to keep us with you when the time comes."

What "the time" was I dared not ask, but I sensed it would not bode well for Montagne, and I endeavored to make myself as unobtrusive as possible in order to overhear all I could. Soon enough I learned that in the past year Drachensbett scouts had discovered a pass across Ancienne (or Drachensbett, as they called the mountain) that could be suitable for an army's passage, should that army be hardened enough to withstand the brutal elements for which the mountain was so infamous. This, clearly, was how Drachensbett's assassins had murdered my mother and uncle, and it was in trailing the assassins that my father had perished. My blood boiled as I remembered King Renaldo's vehement denials. Now Drachensbett, tiring of diplomacy and sensing an opportunity at last to claim the small country in the middle of their own, intended to invade in force, sweeping down the mountain to broach the weaker defenses on Chateau de Montagne's mountain façade.

Much of this I learned by eavesdropping on soldiers frustrated that the attack had not yet occurred. Apparently these plans, drawn for months, had been postponed when news of the ball at Chateau de Montagne had reached their king. (Clever Lord Frederick! He had predicted the ball would delay them.) True to their profession, the soldiers dismissed such politics and now were eager to move. Until orders came, however, they could not, and instead passed their days in endless patrols and military exercises, subsisting on an ever more monotonous diet of beans.

I had never enjoyed beans, no matter how well my mother prepared them. Now my abhorrence of their mushy, pasty tastelessness reached new depths with every meal. Only fear of starvation kept me eating. Chained to my pot, a stinking ram's skin for my bed (I had never known how odiferous wool could be in its natural state, and bristling with twigs and burrs), I fantasized of banquet meals, yearning even for the dry cakes and rubbery aspics so frequent to the table of Chateau de Montagne.

Observing the soldiers dine, I also dreamt, for the first time in my life, of table manners. Packed shoulder to shoulder, the men spat food in their enthusiastic exchanges. They swilled down enormous mouthfuls with equally sizable portions of ale, belched with abandon, and picked their teeth with their knives. I could not tell, in fact, which was more repellent, the food or its consumers, and in my loneliness and revulsion I ached even for Queen Sophia. Envisioning her response to this barbarous spectacle, my spirits rose . . . until I remembered that the queen, whatever her occupation at the moment, was certainly not planning the castle's defense. If only I could warn her!

But no. I was trapped in the camp as surely as a pickle in a pig. Even if I escaped my chains, I could not navigate over the mountain, not before the skilled Drachensbett scouts tracked me down like an animal and dealt me a quick death. That night, huddled on my malodorous sheepskin, my body curled around the flame in my good hand, I begged forgiveness of my father. I had promised to honor him, and instead I was feeding our enemies and polishing their boots as they plotted the capture of Montagne.

I snuffed my flame and not for the first time cried myself to sleep.

✿ ✿ ✿ ✿

Just as a sausage falls from a skillet to the hotter stone below, so too did I discover that however miserable my enslavement had been these many weeks, it was about to become truly unbearable.

As always, the day began with the cook kicking me awake to light his stove, then sending me on my rounds. I crept into each officer's hut more silent than a mouse, for a mouse is not mocked for his "girlish" pink cheeks and soft body, or put to work tugging on officers' boots and brushing their coats, all the time knowing the cook will be waiting with a sharp word and sharper fist for its tardiness.

Inevitably I was late, or late enough, and with a cuff and a curse the cook put me to work at the sink as yet another pot of beans bubbled on the fire. This dismal routine, which normally continued until I collapsed to sleep still damp from the night's last scrubbing, was now broken by a most improbable flourish of horns, followed by great shouts and hurrahs.

The cook at once scuttled to the doorway, his mouth agape. Curious as any other, I peeked around his bony shoulder at a most splendid procession parading through the camp. A dozen fresh soldiers with drummers and pages marched before a handsome young man with fine silver crown, one hand casually holding the reins of his gleaming black mount while the other rested on his thigh. He beamed about, his glee spreading to every man he viewed, so that it took me several moments to connect this face to my former life.

Before, Prince Florian had been all scowls and arrogance in the candlelight; here in the crisp white sun, his cheeks ruddy with cold and his men shouting happy greetings, his haughtiness appeared as glowing poise.

In horror I ducked behind the cook as he passed, for his recognition would be my undoing.

All that day, as the camp swirled in a tempest of activity, I kept out of sight. The prince had little cause to seek out a prisoner of war, but still I evaded him as I scurried about preparing his room and moving the officers. (As a row of dominoes, the colonel was evicted from his quarters to make way for the prince, thus evicting the majors, who demanded the captains' beds, and so on until foot soldiers were left sleeping three abreast.) The camp buzzed with rumor: the prince had some news for all the men to hear at once. Second rounds of patrols were sent after the first, and every soldier spent his spare moments polishing his buttons and combing his hair for the great event.

Alas, my strategy came to naught. Racing from springhead to kitchen, I rounded a corner and collided with the man himself as he examined the pikes of several soldiers.

"Sorry, so sorry," I mumbled, scuttling backwards, water bucket slopping onto my boots.

"Halt!" ordered the prince. "Who might this be?"

I hung my head. It was not my place to address a prince, even if I had desired it.

"Piglet, milord," a soldier answered. "A Montagne boy captured on patrol."

"Truly?" The prince cupped my chin, lifting my head to study my face. I strained not to jerk away as his thumb touched my cheek. "A boy indeed. He's a long way from manhood with that beard . . . You have a face I recognize."

I gulped. "I don't think so. Sir."

"Mmm." He released my jaw. "You could have no relation to the royal family. Perhaps it is simply the resemblance that the people of a nation eventually form."

Bowing low, I crept backwards, resisting the urge to scour away his touch. "Well maintained, especially in this beastly snow," I heard him say of the pikes, his attention already elsewhere, as I turned the corner. Hastily I scrubbed my face with snow, welcoming the rough cold.

The prince had demanded a celebratory feast, the reason for which he would not say, and this news sent the cook into an unprecedented passion that he could vent only on me. I spent hours stoking cook fires, rolling wine barrels, and washing pots. The cook himself produced four great hams from a secret larder, and the sight of them roasting almost set me weeping. So carefully did he watch that I could not steal even a scrap before the first roast was carried to the head table. With a last clout, he sent me after it with a pitcher of wine to guard the soldiers from thirst.

The odor in the mess hall as melting snow mingled with overcooked beans and many male bodies was truly indescribable. Lest we forget, I was not the only camp resident to have gone many weeks without soap. I crept about, pouring wine in the nearest glasses as I did my best not to gag.

At last, the hall packed to bursting, a heaping platter at each place, Prince Florian stood. The soldiers burst into cheers of anticipation.

"Long live the king!" the prince cried, raising his glass.

"Long live the king!" roared back the Drachensbett soldiers, and the men drank deep.

The prince remained standing, a smile on his lips. "As you know, the queen regent of Montagne recently hosted a ball for her niece, the heir apparent, to find her a proper husband. I assure you that the festivities were magnificent, for the castle is a marvel to the eyes, and I know I shall enjoy it immensely."

The men eyed each other, baffled by his confidence. So

closely did I listen that I overfilled a soldier's glass, receiving a kick in response.

"The princess, on the other hand, was quite a different story." Florian's traveling party laughed, apparently familiar with this tale. "A pouting, sullen oaf. I have known barn cats with more grace, and wit, too."

Around the room, men snickered. Lucky I was that no one looked in my direction, else my glare might have smote him dead.

"Be that as it may, she was a small price to pay for the country, and I would have been as happy as any man there to take her hand, onerous as the marriage bed would prove." The men roared with bawdy laughter.

As if sensing my murderous thoughts, Florian caught my eye. "Piglet! Our glasses are empty, boy! Get to work now. Know you the princess?"

I shook my head, eyes down.

"Lucky you are, then. Though the two of you be two toes in a sock, so much are you alike in your voluminous chatter. Don't frown so—I mean no harm by it." He turned back to the crowd. "When I observed that no man could win the princess's favor by charm, I abandoned my intended efforts in that direction, and labored instead as a spy, establishing which of her other suitors I would have to battle for the throne. I danced with several beautiful ladies, and enjoyed in particular a roast quail stuffed with figs. I believe I ate two." He beamed across the room.

The prince, I must concede, was a most talented storyteller, holding every listener in his spell.

"And then, in the midst of my favorite quadrille, a great tumult sounded outside the doors and a guard burst in to announce we were under attack!"

"By who?" a soldier cried out.

"Not by whom—by *what.* A hideous witch had captured Princess Benevolence—from under the very nose of her protectors!—and was attempting to take the girl's life! Queen Sophia herself succeeded in frightening the witch off. I saw the creature myself, sailing through the skies on her broom, cackling like a madwoman!"

(*I was not cackling,* I thought to myself. *I was shrieking in fear!*)

"Where did she go?" asked another soldier.

"I know not. Nor does anyone. She could be . . . anywhere!"

Several men jumped, then chuckled at their fright.

"Well," Florian continued, "this witch had cast a wicked

spell on the princess. The girl could not be awakened, and slept as if dead. Needless to say, dancing halted at once. The queen was quite overcome, and, denying most graciously my father's offer of assistance, sent all guests home that she might grapple undistracted with this tragedy. From far and wide, scholars were queried on how to reverse this dastardly spell. Their universal response? All treatment would be futile, save one." Florian looked around the room, drawing out the moment. "Two days ago, my father received a proclamation from Chateau de Montagne requesting the immediate aid of all young men of royal blood to save the princess, who could be revived only by . . . the kiss of a prince." He beamed again at his men, his narrative concluded.

The soldiers shifted uneasily.

"But sire," the captain queried, "you be one prince among many. Is not your satisfaction premature?"

The prince grinned to split his face. "It is not, my dear man, it is not! For you see, on the day of my birth, a wise woman brought to assist my mother told my fortune. She spoke these exact words, words I would later learn on my father's knee: 'One day your prince shall awaken a princess and win her hand.' Men, such prophesies have power beyond our ability to question or even fully to comprehend. All my life have I awaited this moment. At last it has come. Sheath your swords and unstring your bows, for without a drop of your blood spilling, the kingdom of Montagne shall be ours!"

The low building erupted in cheers. Over and over the prince was toasted and hurrahed. The celebration lasted far into the night, for though the quality of the food by no means suited any banquet as I would define it, the volume of refreshments was unmatched. Wine that had been horded for care of the wounded now flowed freely as the soldiers, absorbing the prince's confidence, rejoiced in their sudden good fortune and the promise that they would soon leave this inhospitable camp for their wives and sweethearts in Drachensbett below.

Much as I wanted to dismiss the prince's words as I scrambled about the hall refilling glasses, I knew I could not. My understanding of the Doppelschläferin spell was in its earliest stages. I had been separated from my double for many weeks already. Could we still reunite, or had the connection between us faded? I did not know, nor did I know whether the prince in fact could revive her. But if he could—and the prophesy, and every tale I had ever read, gave me no reason to believe otherwise—then the bond 'twixt my double and myself would doubtless be severed forever. She, formerly lifeless, would now be princess, while I remained a shepherd boy imprisoned in Drachensbett.

As I valued my life, I must return to my double! Horror at the alternative near set me to hysterics as I toiled late that night, scrubbing dishes and scouring tables. Montagne more than ever required its princess. I had to escape.

I spent sleepless hours struggling through every possible scenario, each more improbable than the previous. At last I fell into fitful slumber, culminating in a most terrifying nightmare. I dreamt I was in my bed chamber in Chateau de Montagne—not my tower cell, but the lovely Peach Rooms—sleeping beneath a down coverlet embroidered with flowers. It being a dream, though sleeping I could yet see, and thus witnessed the arrival of Prince Florian. He entered on tiptoe, a smile on his lips, and as he neared the bed, his face melted into an expression of utmost tenderness. He bent down, shaping his lips into a kiss. I could discern the light glinting on his lashes and his shining eyes, and a curl of hair wrapped around his circlet crown. Closer he came, and closer still. Panic rose in my throat—I thrashed and struggled, but his lips drew ever nearer until they filled all of my vision and blocked all my air.

With a great jerk I awoke, only to find myself face-down

on the fleece, my mouth pressed to filthy wool. I struggled to a seated position, the image of Florian seared with appalling clarity onto my mind's eye. Did I not suffer him enough in waking hours? Had not my parents suffered? Indeed, I considered the dream no small violation of their trust and the vow I had made to avenge their deaths. For many minutes I scrubbed my mouth fiercely, as though scrubbing alone could erase the memory of that kiss.

THIRTEEN

THE NIGHTMARE UNNERVED ME to my core; even the sight of Prince Florian the next morning at breakfast left me vertiginous. But the prince and his entourage paid me no attention whatsoever. As I delivered them yet another platter of hot bacon (a piece of which I managed to hide in my filthy bandages, much to my joy), the captain smacked Florian's shoulder, chuckling. "Seven weeks ago that ball was! To think you've left us shivering up here while you drank and danced about the kingdom—"

"And feasted as well," added Florian with a grin, helping himself to a fistful of bacon. "It's a tough lot, being prince."

Trudging back to the kitchen, I frowned over the captain's words. Seven weeks! Bones could heal in seven weeks' time; that I had learned from my mother. Ducking my head that I might consume my secret treat, I determined to unwrap my dressing as soon as I had a moment to spare.

That time did not come until long past dinner, when at last I was permitted to collapse on my fleece. Doubly exhausted from the day's long efforts and my poor sleep the night before, I nonetheless set to work cutting away the dressing with a knife I had pocketed. The outer wrappings were so caked with grease and dirt that I feared I might skewer myself, but at last I sliced the crucial knots and peeled the rest away.

Twice before I had exposed the wound to ensure it was closing free of corruption. Still, I gagged at the sight. The puncture had healed into an angry red scar made far worse by lack of suturing, though I saw no indication that the bones had not healed. My forearm had shriveled from lack of use, and the skin bore a greasy white film scarcely better than the rags themselves.

With a bit of cloth I wiped at my arm, wishing I had movement enough to manufacture water. Simply flexing my fingers triggered a sharp and lingering ache. I cleaned as best I could, rewrapping my wrist with the scraps of bandage to provide some minimal support. Being careful not to jar it, I settled myself under my cloak.

Yet no sooner had I drifted to sleep, it seemed, than the cook was kicking me awake.

"It's not morning yet!" I protested.

"The prince demands me," he spat out, "and you're to assist."

His skepticism about this arrangement matched my own, and he unlocked my ankle chain with unusual brusqueness. Now I could make out two soldiers stomping their feet at the door. Whatever required the cook's services—or rather the surgeon's, for I suspected the emergency was not of a culinary nature—it must be serious indeed.

The soldiers led us so briskly across the compound that I was forced to trot, and hustled us into the captains' quarters. Inside, a roaring fire (for once not lit by me!) illuminated the prince and two of his aides, the three pacing half-dressed, wringing their hands. Their relief at the cook's entrance was profound, and already I feared the man's skill would not match their expectations.

At once a raking cough filled the hut. So deeply did his bed lay in shadow that I had not seen the captain, his face flushed with fever and exertion. As his coughing continued uncontrollably, the prince turned toward the cook. "Help him!" he implored.

"We'll strip him down," the cook announced. "Open the door now, damn you."

The chill of winter for a man so ill? I could think of countless more appropriate actions. "A mustard plaster would serve better," I blurted out.

The cook spun on me, enraged by my impudence and also, I now recognize, fearful of his own abilities and thus doubly quick to challenge a dull-witted shepherd boy.

As he turned to cuff me, however, the prince stopped him. "Why speak you so?"

I dropped my head, already regretting my words. "My mother always said it. She is—she was—a healer." It pained me to speak so honestly, but I had not time to concoct a fib.

"Why did you not mention this before?"

I shuffled. It was clear, to me at least, that no one had asked, and no one, saving desperation, would have believed it.

But desperate they now were. "Can you assemble such a plaster?" Florian continued.

I nodded.

He turned to the soldiers: "See that he does so! And make haste."

Here I was passing from skillet to stone and hotter stone still. What did I know of mustard plasters? Besides, these were my sworn enemies.

Soon as this last thought crossed my mind, however, I scolded myself. I had spoken out of concern for a fellow human, and shame should I feel for such vindictive thoughts with my mother's name fresh on my lips. Whatever the future held, I vowed, I would marshal my few talents to offer the captain the same care I would any man.

❀ ❀ ❀ ❀

In the days that followed, I scarcely left Johannes's side—for that was the captain's name, and the prince ordered me to use it in the hopes it would provide some solace. The man's condition deteriorated before my eyes, and I struggled to recall my mother's every word, for she had never instructed me as a mistress does her apprentice. In the mess hall, I improvised as best I could, saturating several clean rags with powdered mustard seed and cooking grease. Returning to the sickroom, I placed the potion on Johannes's bare chest that the warmth might soothe his pain and loosen the congestion. The man strained so to breathe that I propped him up with all the bolsters I could find, and I kept the room so hot, a kettle perpetually steaming over the fire, that it was more jungle than mountain hut. To my relief, the cook had a store of dried poppies, and soon as I could I brewed my mother's syrup of boiled poppy heads and honey, for she declared it the single best therapy for cough.

The soldiers sent to guard me quickly changed to lackeys, loading the fire, heating rocks for Johannes's feet, and running for broth and towels at my sharp command. Indeed, had they paused but a moment, they would have wondered at how quickly the servile shepherd boy blossomed into dictator. Further, they should have wondered how his knowledge extended so deep, for healing in both our countries has always been woman's work. But so grateful were all the men that they paid these incriminating facts no heed.

However powerful my disdain for Prince Florian, I must confess that he served his friend most loyally. Given his rank, I could not evict him from the room, much as I longed to do so. My warnings that close proximity might cause his death he brushed aside. Routinely he took a bowl from my hands to feed Johannes himself, and sought my approval prior to every adjustment of the man's bedding.

My discomfort with this situation deepened one evening as the two of us aided Johannes through yet another fit of coughing. When at last the patient quieted, I settled the pillows that he might more comfortably sleep upright, and bathed his forehead with herbal concoctions and aqua vitae as the prince retrieved a fresh compress for his chest. Finishing these tasks at last, I commenced straightening the room so as to avoid my fellow nurse.

"You are blessed, you realize, to have known your mother."

Florian's statement caught me by complete surprise, all the more so as we had worked in silence.

"My mother passed so long ago that I barely remember her," he continued. "What I would give to have known her as you so clearly knew yours."

For a moment I could not speak, even if I had had any notion what to say.

"She called me Florrie. My father used to complain of its girlishness, but she would cover me in kisses . . . ah, I should stop before I set myself weeping."

"I did not know," I whispered.

"That my nickname was Florrie?" He smiled at me.

"That your mother also passed away."

"Yes. We have a bond, the two of us, in our mourning . . . Well, require you my services at the moment? If not, I am afraid I shall have to attend my other responsibilities."

Gently he shut the door behind him, leaving me in such a whirl of emotion that I almost poured a kettle of boiling water on my feet.

Dozing that night on a cot, I dreamt again of the prince and awoke from his kiss with a great jerk as Johannes commenced another spasm of coughing. I rushed to his aid, grateful for the distraction.

❁ ❁ ❁ ❁

My mother, returning once from a particularly difficult case, was asked by my father what the outcome would be. With a weary shrug she replied, "Oh, he'll die or get better. It's always one or the other." To my great relief Johannes did not die and indeed began to show small signs of recovery. Florian, too, noted the improvements, and queried me daily on when the captain might be healthy enough to move. He himself would have departed the camp long before were it not for the "mewling kitten" (as he dubbed Johannes in his earshot) who kept him from his princely duties.

Though I knew far too well what those princely duties entailed, I, too, longed to quit this wretched encampment. Under the pretext of determining how best to transport my patient, I learned that our route to the Drachensbett fortress included a long passage along River Road: the selfsame River Road that climbed the cliff beneath Chateau de Montagne and terminated at the gates of Market Town! Once on this highway, our party mingling with merchant caravans, I could slip away and somehow make my return to Montagne.

However strong my desire, I would not imperil the man whose life I had so recently saved, and I insisted we remain in place until Johannes had strength enough to survive the journey. Daily the camp melted away before my eyes. Soldiers brandishing the tools of carpenter and roustabout reassembled the huts into sledges loaded with provisions, dragged by shaggy horses to the valley below. Platoons of men marched away with songs on their lips, though one of my two lackeys remained in my service. He was essential, I claimed, for carrying trays, as my right hand was still crippled and weak. This was not my only motivation, however, for the man had the build of a bear, and his presence beside me in the kitchen provided absolute protection from the cook's abuse. Indeed, the cook, like all bullies when confronted with a show of force, groveled and fawned before me, producing hidden treats that weeks earlier I would have killed to acquire but now had not time to eat. Instead I rushed them to Johannes's bed in the hopes that some morsel would inspire his appetite.

One evening, bringing my patient some small delicacy, I discovered the captain sharing a flagon of wine with Florian. The two looked as guilty as truants upon my appearance, and Florian even made to hide the container beneath a blanket.

"Forgive us, O Noble Healer. But is it not true that the fruit of the vine cures the ill?"

Such a relief it was to see the captain sitting up, and thirsty, that I could not restrain a smile. "Well, they do say that a diet of drink leads to debauchery," I pointed out.

"Ah, debauchery," murmured the captain.

Florian chuckled. "Clearly you are improving, my friend! We must return you to the wenches—they will cure you in their own way."

"That they would. I dream of Rosalind and her soft *pillows.* She is a delectable lass and would give herself to you in a heartbeat. She asks after you every time we frolic together."

Never in all my sheltered life had I heard men speak so! My face burned in mortification, and I longed to race from the building, at least to plug my ears against this bawdy candor . . . but, I reminded myself, no *boy* would behave so prudishly. All I could do was bite my lip and pray the conversation ended soon.

"I do not doubt Rosalind does," the prince said with a

laugh. "But it is the crown that catches her eye, not the face beneath it. No, I would never take advantage so. Far better she keep her heart for her own true love, whoever he may be."

"You are far too chivalrous, my prince, with all your prattling on true love."

"Prattle! I take offense. What think you, Ben, on the subject?"

The two men, turning in my direction, burst into laughter at my embarrassment.

Florian grinned. "Clearly he has not savored the pleasures of his own young shepherdess . . . But surely you agree, Ben, that the bond between two hearts is the greatest satisfaction a man and woman can ever know."

My cheeks flushed to an even darker red as I stuttered out a useless answer.

"Stop or you shall slay him, and then no one shall be left to care for me," said Johannes. As if to demonstrate, he began to cough, which to my great relief terminated their salacious nattering. I struggled some minutes to make him comfortable, and then the combination of wine and exertion quickly put him to sleep.

"He is like a brother to me," Florian whispered, gazing at

his friend with true affection. "Indeed, more than once my father informed me that had he known our two characters, he would have switched us at birth."

Much as I struggled, I could think of no reply. Their earlier conversation, combined with the revelation of the prince's romantic nature—shocking to me, and completely unpredicted—had left me incapable of coherent thought.

"Yet again, Johannes serves as example. We should both of us rest. Sleep well, Ben."

I lay abed many hours that night, working at my stiff fingers and wrist until the pain near drove me mad, but the agony served to keep me awake. At last, however, sleep enveloped me. As I feared, Prince Florian appeared in my dreams yet again. Settling himself on the edge of my Peach Room bed, he took my hand and brought it to his lips with the warmest of smiles. "Jest with me, sweet Princess. Awake, that we might frolic together." He leaned forward—

I lunged awake with a shriek. Panting, I listened for pounding footsteps. Surely my scream had awakened the camp! But the dark silence was broken only by the captain's snore. I must have dreamt the scream as well.

Pulling my cloak about me, I crawled to the fire and relit it with a quick gesture. I would not sleep again this night.

Instead, huddled by the coals, I plotted the details of my escape. Tomorrow, whatever Johannes's condition, we must depart.

❀ ❀ ❀ ❀

Depart we did, in a company of soldiers and horsemen. I had intended Johannes to ride in a sledge, but with the enthusiasm of recovery he declared that he would sooner set himself afire than occupy that insult, and insisted on joining us on horseback. The bright sunshine, I had to admit, did him good, and the men's cheers as he mounted brought a smile to his pale features.

I myself had my own troubles, having never before ridden astride. Fortunately my mount proved in both gait and temperament more rocking chair than warhorse, but remaining upright took much of my concentration, and my imminent escape the remainder. Oh, how I longed to see again my beloved castle, and my Doppelschläferin. I yearned even for grim Sophia, whom in a fever of homesickness I swore I would never again disobey.

Descending the mountain, we passed from snow to flowers and soft grass, bleating lambs and twittering songbirds. Yet beyond these vernal displays, the countryside bore little resemblance to Montagne. The farms had a hardscrabble quality, and the rugged terrain lent itself less generously to agriculture. Now could I understand why the Drachensbett forever sought possession of its more fertile neighbor.

The hardships of his native land certainly had no effect on the prince, for he grew cheerier and more boisterous with every bend in the trail. For a time he sang a bawdy ditty about a shepherd girl (winking at me as he belted out these lines) and the mountain goat who loved her. The soldiers joined each chorus with raucous enthusiasm.

"So, young Ben," he asked, falling in beside me and the captain, "you have no taste for song today?"

"No, Your Highness. Or skill."

"Oh, anyone can sing a song as dreadful as this! I realize now I have never plucked your brain for information on your fair country."

"There's nothing to pluck." I shrugged, feigning nonchalance.

"That I cannot believe. Surely men have commented on your resemblance to the princess—though you are far cleverer and more interesting, I can assure you."

Inwardly I gritted my teeth at this insult.

"What of that gorgon, the queen regent? Have you ever felt her claws?"

Johannes chuckled. "Tell the story—you must. It grows richer on every recitation."

"Oh, doubtless Ben has heard. Of course you know of King Ferdinand's death last spring. Another perished as well, I believe."

Too pained to speak at this casual mention of my mother, I did not respond.

"Perhaps you know as well that my father, on learning this dreadful news, offered every condolence to Ferdinand's widow. Though our two countries have a complex history, the tragedy affected him deeply, for he has always held the queen in highest regard, and we made haste to arrive in time for the king's interment."

Such euphemism! Does a "complex history" include invasion, treachery, assassination?

In his enthusiastic recitation, the prince paid my distress no heed. "Following the ceremony, my father begged leave to speak with the queen, and there, before her court, he offered with the greatest consideration to scour the mountain for the beast that had committed this horrible deed."

I could not contain myself. "Beast? You mean a dragon?"

"But of course." He feigned surprise. "What else explains this killing? Oh, do not look upon me with such outrage! Behold, Johannes, his face quite resembles the queen's."

"Indeed it does, Your Highness." The captain smiled, enjoying this immensely.

"His reaction only adds to my story. Now, Ben, take that emotion you so clearly demonstrate, add to it the tongue of a viper and the wit of a most diabolic muse, and you would have the queen. Never in my life have I experienced such suffering as I did then."

"As did we all," Johannes chuckled.

"Yes, I concede it." Florian now produced an admirable caricature of Sophia's measured tones. "'A dragon, you say?'—speaking to my father, the king of Drachensbett, as a mistress might address a negligent maid!—'Have you yourself set eyes on this *dragon?*' My father was forced to concede that he had not. 'Has any member of the party assembled before us espied this alleged creature?' We all shook our heads. 'Has any of you come across tracks, eggs, dens, fewmets, caches, or any other indication that this beast not only exists but occupies the mountain of Ancienne?'"

By this point the captain was biting his glove to restrain

his laughter, and soldiers crowded about, straining to hear Florian's tale.

"I must confess I am relieved the woman serves as queen rather than general! She completed this interrogation, leaving us shuffling and staring at our feet; I was, at least. Finally she spoke, so softly that I did not at first recognize the depth of her fury. 'You come before our court—you, who have striven time and again to claim our lands and exterminate our people—not a day after the most brutal and cowardly slaying of our beloved ruler, and present as explanation for this singularly heinous crime a creature that not one of you has ever witnessed, that you have no proof of whatsoever beyond picture books and the gossiping chatter of old men. We are in mourning! Adorned in black, we grapple to perceive the future that awaits us, and with all due respect we say to you—to you, whom a child of four would identify as the prime if not only suspects in this most brutal offense—that your presence in our chambers represents a jeering mockery of every value we hold dear, and we beg you to depart ere a second regicide bloody our soil.'" Finishing, Florian settled back with a slight bow.

"Well remembered, sir," murmured a soldier as others exchanged grins.

Florian eyed me. "So, what think you now of your ruler?"

"That she well deserves the throne," I answered. Never before had I spoken in Sophia's defense, and yet I spoke these words with all my heart.

Johannes stiffened, but the prince waved him away. "How could he know?"

"About dragons?" I asked, and was stunned to see a dozen men nod. "You truly believe there are dragons on Ancienne?"

"It is their bed," a soldier muttered.

"So you find the queen's speech amusing because you think she is *wrong?*"

"Calm yourself, little Ben," said the prince. "You cannot help that you and your countrymen inhabit a world of illusion—"

Finally, irreparably, I snapped. For weeks I had borne the cruelty and indignities of a hundred enemy soldiers. Suffering through cold, deprivation, the throbbing ache of my arm, and the incapacity of my hand, I had held my tongue. Even the prince's teasing jabs, his ribaldries and mocking, could not set me off. But his casual insult of my mother, his insistence against all evidence that the Badger Tragedy had been perpetrated by a creature of fantasy, and finally his unwelcome and wholly disquieting presence in my dreams, these had at last driven from me all prospect of self-control.

"A world of illusion?" I spat out. "And where, I beg, do you reside?"

"I know not to what you refer—"

"You—has no one ever told the prince of Drachensbett that he lives in a world of *delusion?*"

Several soldiers reached for their swords. "Careful, Ben . . ." warned Johannes.

"You speak of true love, dear prince—that all men, and women, too, should know their heart's desire. And yet even now, those words fresh on your lips, you set off to claim a princess whom you yourself describe as a sullen and graceless oaf. When you jested of the obligations of the marriage bed, you could not suppress a shiver, so revolting did you find her."

The prince glared at me, taut with anger. "If you value your life, seal your lips at once."

"*That* is the delusion of which I speak! You wish the joys of true love upon every milkmaid and stable boy in your land, and yet you consign yourself and another to lives of pure misery that you might possess a well-proportioned ballroom."

"Enough!" roared the prince. "I will not tolerate such insubordination, such . . . such lies, such terrible lies! Tomorrow I meet my destiny. When I return, I shall see you hung."

At once heavy gloves snatched me from my mount and bound me in chains. Never once for the remainder of our journey did the prince look at me, or indeed at anyone, but only drove his horse forward, lashing at the branches of every tree he encountered.

As for myself, instead of escaping my captors on the River Road, I traveled it gagged and flopping in the bottom of a cart, cursing my stupidity.

FOURTEEN

So it transpired that I spent the night ere Prince Florian departed to claim my hand locked in the bowels of the Drachensbett fortress, my life as good as finished. The following morn, the prince would ride to Montagne, awaken the Doppelschläferin, and at once take her and the nation for his own. If it emerged that the Doppelschläferin had not a wit in her head—given the original from which she sprang, I had no reason to believe otherwise—it would make little difference to the prince, for he was entering the union with the lowest of expectations. Perhaps with minor effort he could convince her even of the existence of dragons, so credible was the man's act. I, on the other hand, the true princess, faced public execution. Perhaps—and such was my mood that I considered this a cheery thought—I could beg for release atop Ancienne. Then I might rediscover the icy cavern that entombed my father and there join him in death. Centuries hence, an explorer would discover our petrified corpses. If I had time ere I perished, I would carve my full name, and his, into the stone . . .

No! Such thoughts, mesmerizing though they might be, served me no purpose. I must escape this dungeon. Despondently I surveyed my cell: several rusted rings embedded in the walls, a scrap of hay for bedding, and a high barred window. In desperation I threw myself against the heavy wooden door, bemoaning my measly gift of fire. Anything would serve me better—a trebuchet or shrieking banshee, a blacksmith forge to melt the lock—

I blinked. I could make fire, and if my other hand, still stiff and aching, cooperated, wind as well. Were these not the two components of a forge?

At once I stripped off my cloak.

It took half the night to draw a gust from my fingertips. My arm soon throbbed so painfully that I feared I had cracked the bones anew. At last I produced a breeze, my panic transforming the wind into a veritable gale, and with it coaxed the fire in my other hand to searing heat. The door at once began to burn, filling my cell with smoke. No matter how I tried, though, I could not produce a flame hot enough to melt iron, however much the wood around it flamed and charred.

Half mad with frustration, coughing and gagging in the stink, I pounded on the door. Its underpinnings burnt away, the lock shifted and fell with a clatter onto the floor.

Well, then. Recipes rank less than results. Donning my cloak, I cracked open the door. Wood smoke poured into the dank passageway, and hastily I shut the door behind me. Creeping around a corner, I caught sight of the exit . . . and a bulky guard filling the stairwell as he dozed against his staff. Quick as I could, I formed a rock in my hands—well, more sand than rock, so poor my technique—and tossed it past him. Incompetent at all sports, I sent the lure far wide of its mark, but the commotion nonetheless roused the man, who, guilty and befuddled, wandered off to find its source. Alone, I dashed up the stairs to the main hall.

I struggled to retrace my earlier tumultuous journey through the fortress. How different the space now appeared, resting in that quiet interlude when one day passes seamlessly to the next. Three soldiers, arguing monotonously over the attributes of different varieties of apples, paid no heed whatsoever to the figure creeping through the shadows and slipping ghostlike through the main doors.

Once outside, I was confronted with an even more intimidating challenge. Somehow I must breach those mammoth walls, locate myself a fleet-footed creature, and race to Montagne, arriving at all costs before the prince. Unfortunately I had no notion how to escape this edifice, or wealth to purchase or skill to steal such a mount. The illustration of the handless sorcerer who had attempted to use his magic for profit sprang to mind. Having only recently regained some small use of my hand, I had no interest whatsoever in losing both limbs forever. But perhaps . . . Would it be acceptable to create *false* wealth?

Hurriedly I located a mound of refuse that glittered most encouragingly. With momentous effort, singeing my fingertips countless times, I succeeded in melting those fragments of wine bottles into a half-dozen green . . . Well, to be honest, they did not much resemble emeralds. In fact, they most evoked insect larvae. Even I, their creator, was slightly repulsed. Yet they were all I had. Grasping my faux gems with as much resolve as I could muster, I tiptoed through the shadows toward the fortress gates.

As roosters battled cacophonously for domination of the dawn, a night-soil wagon crossed my path, rattling and dripping. I gagged at the smell. As the driver paused for a marching platoon, I realized with a sigh of disgust that the vehicle offered an ideal means of escape. Just as the last soldier passed the front of the wagon, I slipped between its rear wheels, clinging to its crossbeams and praying with all my strength that I would not be discovered.

Had I attempted this exercise at any other point in my life I should have failed, but weeks of slavery had strengthened me immeasurably. Even so, my injured hand could scarcely bear my weight. Night soil oozed onto my cloak, and I wondered why all my adventures involved foul odor. Why could I not for once frolic in a meadow of flowers, or escape in a hamper of fresh laundry? No, I must endure night soil and prison cells and unwashed soldiers . . .

So occupied, I barely noticed our passage through the gates, and only when the wagon jerked through a sizable puddle, dousing me with chilly water, did I realize we had reached the main road. At least, I consoled myself, dropping into the mud, the wet would remove some of the stink. I had not changed clothes or bathed since my capture, and my short locks were as matted and greasy as sheep's wool. After scrubbing my hands and face, and rinsing the worst of my cloak's soilings, I set off at once for Montagne.

Though Drachensbett is thrice the size of Montagne, its capital lies only half a day's ride from Chateau de Montagne; this I knew already. I now learned a second, bitter truth: the

River Road as it winds through Drachensbett is completely devoid of horse merchants and emergency mounts, particularly at dawn. The farther I trudged, in fact, the rarer became settlements of any kind. At one point a merchant passed with a string of donkeys. When he saw what I offered for their purchase, however, he informed me with language that stained the air what he thought of my bits of glass, and me as well.

The sun rose, birds sang their songs of love, but all for naught. I would never reach Montagne in time. Despondent, I approached a peasant boy leading a cow. "Do you happen to know where I could get a horse?" I asked wearily.

"Ah, no. But I'm selling this one here," came the answer.

I studied the sweet-faced creature. "Can I ride her to Montagne this morn?"

The boy laughed. "No, but she'll give you cream enough if you treat her right."

Knowing I would receive another refusal, I held out my damp handful of glass. "Can I buy her for this?"

The boy's eyes grew wide. "They be magic, right?"

I nodded and, wincing, uttered the first lie that entered my head: "They're beans."

"Can I have them all?" he begged.

"Of course." At once we concluded our business and I led my new purchase down the road, the boy racing off in the other direction. What became of him, I do not know, but to this day I think of him with gratitude.

Approaching the first farmhouse in sight, I at once exchanged the cow for a saddle and a mangy, knock-kneed nag unaccustomed to the pace I demanded of her. I struggled as best I could, forcing the old mare onward by pleadings and kicks as I continually checked behind me, attempting to catch sight of Florian and his ilk among the merchants and travelers now filling River Road.

Ancienne loomed ever larger until the mountain's sheer northern face filled half the sky. Rounding a bend, I could make out Chateau de Montagne on the far horizon, and my heart swelled with pride at my ancestors' genius, the brilliance of the castle's placement. Even from this distance I could discern the slender profile of the Wizard Tower. What an act of desperate bravado that had been, my plunge from that window! I remembered it as ancient history, yet not three months had elapsed since that fateful night.

Now could I see the waterfall's mist, and the switchbacks that carried travelers up the ridge into Montagne. My mare and I were both drenched from the effort of forcing her forward. Well it was that I kept a rearward eye, for at the foot of the ridge, I espied a large and brilliantly colored party cantering up the center of the road. Had I met them on the switchbacks, all would have been lost. As it was, I had just time enough to drag my perspiring nag into the ditch, keeping her body between myself and the passing cavalcade, Florian in the midst of horns and banners and tinkling bells.

The moment they left my sight, I raced to follow them. Here I encountered a severe setback, for my ill-tempered mare, once free of her demanding burden, had no intent of permitting my remount, and I was not equestrian enough to force the matter. At last, having battled her for some time in a manner most amusing to passersby, I called surrender and, sending her off to find green pastures, hurried up the switchbacks on foot.

By the time I crested the top I could barely draw breath, so demanding that ascent. But my efforts were at once rewarded, for through my ragged gasps I perceived the glorious mass of Chateau de Montagne, and beyond it the entrance to Market Town, teeming with merchants, country folk, and travelers.

Doing my best to look the part of shepherd, I inserted myself into a family driving lambs to market. The group barely acknowledged my presence, so busy were they with their daunting task, and preoccupied, I am sure, by the promising spectacle of an afternoon's holiday. Yet their company, such as it was, saw me safely into town.

Hiding my face deep beneath my hood, for I was now amid people who had known me all my life, I hastened through the streets to the castle. Here, too, I found fortune, for the guards at the gate paid me no heed, instead giving all their attention to the Drachensbett party that gazed about the inner courtyard in a most offensively proprietary manner.

Slipping through the gates, I crept along the courtyard's perimeter. I was not halfway to my destination, however, when I was detected. "It's Piglet!" a Drachensbett soldier shouted, and as one they sprinted toward me: my escape must have been ill received. However slowly I had trod before, my boots now barely touched the cobblestones, and I attained speeds I would never have imagined possible. Reaching an alley just ahead of their grasping hands, I rounded the corner and dove like a rabbit through the crumbling bas-relief hedgehog.

My head smashed against the far side of the passageway with force enough to bring stars to my eyes. I struggled to silence my wheezing cries. Only an arm's reach away, the men paced and raged at my disappearance, cursing each other for losing me. My throbbing skull, and the stitch in my side as well, were a small price indeed for this spectacle, and my face broke into the first true smile I had known in months. My task was near complete—at my tormentors' expense, no less! I had only to find my double and return at last to my life as princess.

❀ ❀ ❀ ❀

Easier said than done, I soon realized, for I had no idea where my double lay. Though moderate for a castle, Chateau de Montagne is quite large enough, and Florian was inside already, approaching ever nearer his supposed bride.

Through secret passageways I raced, not caring who should hear my pounding feet. Where would she be? My pretty little bedroom—etched in my dreams—was empty, as was the throne room, the ballroom, the great hall crowded with castle staff whispering in twos and threes—

Passing a corridor, I espied Lord Frederick on the edge of a chair, the queen pacing the rug beside him. With every pore of their beings they conveyed fearful anticipation, and I knew I must be close.

There, in the next room, lay my Doppelschläferin—but too late! For Prince Florian was bent already over her sleeping form. The buttons and epaulets of his uniform gleamed, and sunlight glinted on curl and crown.

I watched, horror-struck. He leaned closer—

And stepped back. Clearly I was witnessing, if not a failure of nerve, at least a measured consideration of the many consequences his action would soon provoke. With a long and heartfelt exhalation he walked to the window and lay his head against the glass.

The queen in her cunning had selected, I now saw, the most appropriate chamber of all the castle in which to present her enchanted niece. Known only as the Blue Room, it was small but faultless. Brocade of palest blue and gold curtained the windows; the walls were covered with pale blue silk, and the few simple furnishings lent an elegance to the space that the Drachensbett fortress would never know. From the window where Prince Florian now stood, lost in thought, one could see the courtyard below, impeccable in its proportions, the charming mélange of Market Town, and the Montagne valley, lush and green in its verdant mantle.

My double, too, had been placed to best advantage. She

was dressed yet in the ball gown and wig I remembered all too well, her plump hands on her chest and a spot of rouge on her cheeks. Yet even in her enchanted sleep, a small frown creased her forehead, and I could not but wonder if it was this sullen appearance that gave the prince pause.

His hesitation, however, would prove my salvation. I stripped off my garments, for I had not a second to spare. Wrapping myself in my cloak, not daring even to draw breath, I tiptoed through the portal. To my great good fortune, the prince appeared far too preoccupied to register my faint noise. A step—step—step—and I reached the Doppelschläferin. With a last cautious glance at Florian, I tossed the cloak through the portal and dove into the body.

My double lurked closer to death than I had realized. For several desperate moments I could not draw breath. Panic rose in my throat. I felt entombed in living rock—I labored and fought, willing my way back to life . . .

And then, with a jerk, I awoke. Not inches from my face was Prince Florian, his eyes shut, bitter resignation clouding his visage, and his lips squeezed in a most disdainful pucker.

Once again, my own lips proved my undoing: "Don't you dare."

The prince leapt back with a cry. Wild-eyed, he stared at

me, and waves of horror and recognition crossed his face. "Ben! Benevolence! You are—you were—"

"I *am,*" I inserted. "I am Ben."

"No . . . No, no, no!" He sprang for the door, and almost at once I heard the mad clatter of hoofbeats as he galloped from the courtyard, his men following in confusion behind him.

FIFTEEN

Silence permeated Chateau de Montagne. My many trials, culminating in my most perilous escape from Drachensbett and two nights without sleep, had drained me completely. Perhaps the weakness of my Doppelschläferin contributed as well, though I am not expert enough in such matters to speak with authority. Whatever the cause, my race to the window to watch this dramatic departure depleted the last of my strength. Sophia burst into the room just as I collapsed onto the carpet.

How many times in the past weeks had I dreamt of the castle! How often had I longed even for Sophia. Now my eyes fluttered open—only to find the queen looming over me, her hand poised to slap my face.

"She has awakened, Your Majesty!" Lord Frederick cried, clutching her arm.

The queen was not *punishing* me, I realized with a hot surge of relief; she was merely attempting my resuscitation.

"Praise the heavens!" she exclaimed. "The prince revived her."

"No," I murmured. "He did not. I . . . I revived myself."

The queen spun about, focusing on me as a cat might attend an active mouse hole. "What is this? The prince had no role?"

"No," I whispered, the room spinning before my eyes.

"Are you quite certain?" she pursued, again looking ready to strike me in her eagerness for information.

Lord Frederick interjected. "Tell us, dear princess, how we might best assist you."

I swallowed weakly. "I am . . . so very, very hungry."

Frantic as she was to learn more of my interaction with Florian, the queen at least recognized my basic requirements. She hastily called an order for sustenance and demanded two strong footmen transport me to my bed.

Carried into the Peach Rooms radiant in the spring sunlight, I beamed with happiness. Once I had despised these chambers; now I cherished them with all my heart.

"We—the need is no longer—" The queen appeared

genuinely embarrassed. "Given the trauma of the past months, and of course our fear of witches, it may be safest here—"

She misinterpreted my joy! How could I explain, particularly in my dazed state, that I would have been delighted to return even to my cold and barren cell, so long as I was back in my true home and far from Drachensbett?

"Thank you, Your Majesty" was all that I could manage. A tray appeared, heavy with tarts and creams, miniature tender vegetables, bonbons of all assortments, a pitcher of hot chocolate and, last of all, a steaming cassoulet of lamb and tender white beans.

Catching sight of this dish, I collapsed into hysterical giggles. So long did I laugh that the observers who crowded my bedroom must certainly have considered me mad, however pleasant the madness seemed. Avoiding the beans with care, I worked my way through the tray, though my stomach, empty from my day of flight and emptier still after two months of grim camp fare, had little capacity. At once exhaustion suffused me, and though the queen ached to hear what had transpired in the Blue Room, neither she nor Lord Frederick could extract a single word from my lips, and so left me to a sleep more luxurious and appreciated than any I had ever known.

❀ ❀ ❀ ❀

I slumbered without interruption through the afternoon and all the night, and when I awoke at last, I felt as refreshed as the goddess of dawn herself. Dawn, indeed, had already passed, and for a time I luxuriated between my soft sheets, marveling at every detail of my chamber with a fresh and most grateful eye. In my absence, a dove had constructed a nest on the windowsill, and her soft cooing proved most delightful.

Admiring her song, I picked out different, jarring tones as well. At last curiosity conquered sloth, and I stepped to the window that I might identify the source of this discordance.

The noises that so disturbed my rest, I saw now, had been nothing less than the rattle of sword against armor, the twanging test of bow strings, and the stomp of soldiers preparing their stations. About the battlements, archers settled between parapets with their crossbows at the ready, focusing all their attention on the portcullis creaking upward. At last the creaking ended and through that formidable opening rode ten black-uniformed soldiers, and then—

I clutched the sill for support as Prince Florian himself appeared astride his black stallion, surveying the castle in sullen contempt. Gray-bearded men followed behind.

Florian's arrival could mean one thing alone: the demand of my hand. If that was the case, I had to know so as to prepare with all possible speed my defense. I locked the door and located at once a portal behind a hand-painted etching of a hedgehog. Wherever the prince and his minions had been escorted, I would follow, and through the veil of magic observe all that I could of my enemy.

I trotted the narrow passageways, marveling at the newfound comfort of my ball gown. My time as prisoner must have raised my tolerance for pain, or perhaps my relief at returning to Montagne suppressed it. Whatever the explanation, I navigated the passages with a lightness of foot I had never before experienced.

As I suspected, the Drachensbett contingent had been delivered to the throne room. I arrived at my secret portal in time to witness their formal greeting of the queen, the prince glowering and sulky.

"We welcome you to Chateau de Montagne, dear neighbors," Sophia intoned, "and we confess our curiosity as to the meaning of this visit."

The eldest statesman—so I deduced by his appearance and respectful acknowledgment of Lord Frederick—stepped forward. "Your Most Royal Majesty, members of the court, honored burghers"—the guild masters were present as well! I had not noticed, and took the occasion more seriously still—"I am sent as messenger by Renaldo, King of Drachensbett. As you know, the throne of Montagne, while ably guarded by Sophia, Queen Regent, by law and tradition shall pass to her niece, the Princess Benevolence, upon the girl's majority. A powerful spell placed upon the princess left her as dead until yesterday—"

"We did not kiss!" Prince Florian hissed, unable to contain himself. "Nor shall we ever!"

Florian's interruption, his unprecedented disrespect and rancorous scowl, stunned the court.

The ambassador shifted, adjusting his collar. "Ahem. Yes. Be that as it may, the princess's recovery now raises other issues. The obligations of my position and my monarch require I point out that the princess has not, and I fear will never, display the qualities essential to a head of state."

Hidden on the far side of the portal, I fumed and squirmed. Bad enough that I must listen to this searing criticism, but his presentation to the entire Montagne court—some of its members nodding their agreement!—wounded me beyond measure.

"Her apathy, languor, and gluttony, her patent disregard for the obligations of her rank and future position—all of which she displayed at the winter's festivities in a manner unforgettable to observers—these liabilities lead to one conclusion: that the ancient nation of Montagne will suffer grievously, and perhaps perish altogether, should she rule." The ambassador drew a breath. "Therefore my king, seeking the security and well-being of the populace of this fair country, makes a Claim of Benevolent Succession to this throne."

Benevolent succession? I had never heard the term. From the anxiety that flashed across the face of Lord Frederick, however, he knew it all too well.

The ambassador waited. Sophia looked to Lord Frederick.

"Greatly we appreciate your solicitous concern for our people," the man began at last. "Benevolent succession, however, is a most serious matter, determining the fate of every man and woman among us, and I beg time to consider your claim ere we reply."

The ambassador nodded. "I could ask nothing less, were I in your position. Shall two months be period enough?"

Lord Frederick turned to his queen, but she remained as a statue. "We would prefer four," he answered at last. "We shall use them wisely."

With more bows and flourishes, the Drachensbett ambassadors withdrew. Soon as the door closed behind them, the queen spoke. "We would be alone. Frederick?"

In small knots of worried discussion, the lords and ladies and burghers made their way from the throne room until only Sophia and her most trusted advisor remained.

"What, pray tell, is benevolent succession?" demanded the queen, free at last to pace off her wrath.

"It is, Your Majesty, a most dreadful turn of events. Many centuries ago, the countries of this region settled upon the practice. When, as in our current condition, the heir to the nation provokes . . . concern, and no other heir exists, a neighboring kingdom may claim the throne as theirs, absorbing the land without bloodshed, revolution, or anarchy."

"And the absorbed nation permits this?"

"If the alternative be anarchy, yes. The claim is never made casually, and the threatened country may demand independent assessment of the heir in question."

"As if assessment would work in our favor," the queen sniffed. "We are a sovereign nation! We shall reject at once such impertinence!"

Lord Frederick shook his head sadly. "No Claim of Benevolent Succession has been tendered for more than a hundred years; such is its gravity. But when last a claim was made, one hundred thirty-two years ago, and a nation no larger than ours rejected it, the Baron of Farina, being so snubbed by the good people of Alpsburg, attacked the country and burnt every building in it to the ground." He paused to collect his breath, and to wipe a tear from his eye. "Your Majesty, I fear we are doomed."

❧ ❧ ❧ ❧

Burnt every building to the ground. The lord's words rang in my ears, and my own tears flowed at his hopeless resignation. I stumbled blindly through the passageways, the joy that had so recently filled me now vanished as a drop of water vanishes in a mighty conflagration. Poor Montagne! That my lovely beloved country should be crushed under the boot of Drachensbett! The temerity, the boasting, cowardly imperiousness of those awful men . . . To kill my family, laying the blame on dragons or pixies or whatever fantastical creature seemed most appropriate to finger, then plot an infiltrating attack across the mountains—pausing only to determine first if the throne might be taken bloodlessly, and heartlessly, via my hand—then furthermore, not a day after failing to claim me through an obscure and questionable prophesy, to degenerate to a most ancient and brutal institution that they might take Montagne as their own . . . How dare they! How dare!

Ensnarled in my thoughts, I howled in frustration, startling two guards in the Hall of Flags, which I happened to be passing at the moment. Marvelous. Now rumors of witchcraft would resume as well. That wretched benevolent succession. Benevolent, indeed! It be more devilry than kindness. And to think *my* name, my given name, and that awful term coincided! Insult heaped upon insult.

Arriving at my bedroom, I collapsed into a dusty tangle of brocade and despair. Uninvited, my dreams of Prince Florian's entrance to this room came to mind, his tender expression of care and delight. How profound the contrast between that handsome face and his present scowl, or his disdainful appearance yesterday as he had struggled to kiss the enchanted figure before him.

At once the words that I had labored so hard to hold back now flooded my consciousness, those awful, searing terms with which the Drachensbett ambassador had impugned every aspect of my being: apathetic, slothful, dim . . . I could not remember every particular criticism, but the gist of his indictment, accepted by the entire Montagne court without even an attempt at my defense, was without doubt the most horrific insult I could ever imagine.

And yet, as I lay sobbing on the carpet, a small part of me could not but admit that the words, savage though they might have been, were not, alas, untrue. If one's sole opportunity to determine my character came about at the ball, what other conclusion could be drawn? That night I had behaved as a sulky and self-pitying imbecile. Since arriving in the castle a year ago, I had not once (my sobs intensified as I considered each damning scene) displayed the slightest ability for or inclination toward the responsibilities of royalty. To be sure, the curriculum through which I suffered could scarce inspire enthusiasm in even a conscientious princess. Yet my flagrant dismissal of every aspect of court life would lead the most sympathetic of observers to determine that I was unfit in every way for the crown.

Through the lush carpet, I could sense footsteps approaching. The bedroom door rattled, and instinctively I huddled closer to the floor.

"Ben?" Hildebert called. "Unlock this door, now."

"No!" I answered, my sobs returning in force. "Go away!"

Is that how a princess acts? whispered a voice inside my head. I sobbed louder, but my conscience, now awakened, was not so easily suppressed. *Remain there sobbing, and you'll fulfill all Drachensbett's predictions.*

"Silence!" I hissed. "I am weary! I have suffered—cannot you see that?"

Poor thing, murmured my conscience in a most irritating manner.

With a resentful sigh, I sat up. "Just a moment," I called to Hildebert. "I need to—to freshen up."

"Shall I begin your bath?" she asked.

"Ah . . . yes."

That would be quite considerate of you, prodded my conscience.

"That would be quite considerate of you," I continued, though I could not help rolling my eyes.

"Oh—thank you, Your Highness. 'Tis very nice of you to say so."

I flushed with shame at Hildebert's gratitude. Plainly I had not paid her adequate courtesy.

I stumbled to the looking glass. With greasy and tangled curls atop a pouting, tear-smeared face, I looked truly abominable. Never had a girl less resembled a princess. And yet, despite my appearance, I could not be as awful as that Drachensbett monster had made out. I must have some redeeming qualities . . .

At once, a thought struck me. Lord Frederick had said the Claim of Benevolent Succession could be voided if the heir in question was gauged to be competent. Despite all my public misconduct, in the past year I had learned the Elemental Spells, the Doppelschläferin, and the preparation and flying of a magic broom; I had survived two months as prisoner of war, saving the life of the captain Johannes in the process; I had escaped the dungeons of Fortress Drachensbett, and after an arduous journey successfully reunited with my double, so preserving her, and all Montagne, from Prince Florian's rapacity. As ever my life mattered, and the lives of my people, I would somehow master the despicable art of being a princess.

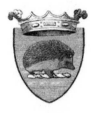

Part Four

In which my greatest horror is narrowly avoided,

and then most pleasantly comes to pass

SIXTEEN

MY FIRST CHALLENGE as a resolute young princess arrived not five minutes after my heartfelt vow. I entered the adjoining room as Hildebert finished drawing my bath, and stood as always that she might release me from the ball gown and multitudinous undergarments that had encased my body, or one of them, these past months. The woman had tact enough, given my recent hysterics, not to inquire as to how I had covered myself in dust. Nonetheless, she scowled and tsked as she removed my gown, crinolines, and petticoats, and could not suppress a gag as the true strength of my unwashed body reached her nose.

"They never mentioned this part of the enchantment," she muttered, unlacing my corset. She knelt to unroll my stockings, and gasped. "Your Highness, what's happened to you?"

"Whatever do you mean—?" I began, and caught sight of my reflection. Clad only in a short chemise, my limbs exposed, I could see myself—or rather, what was left of myself, for I had half melted away. Was this some horrific aftermath of the Doppelschläferin spell? Would I soon disappear altogether?

"You've slimmed up, that you have," said Hildebert.

Of course! My two months in Drachensbett, with its backbreaking labor and monotonous diet, and perhaps as well the Doppelschläferin's long isolation, had serendipitously produced the very silhouette about which Queen Sophia so incessantly hounded me. Not that I was slender, certainly, but where once I had bulged out, now I dipped ever so slightly inward.

Unsure as to how to react to this singular turn of events, I settled on the one truth I could establish: "I'd best begin washing."

Alone in my tub, I soon had privacy to marvel. The merger of my two halves had yet again produced a peculiar amalgam. Where yesterday a raw red welt the size of my thumb had blighted my forearm, I now had only the palest of scars, though the arm was as stiff and sore as ever. (Indeed, it would be many months before my hand came near its previous mobility, and ever after my arm would ache at the approach of foul weather.) My hair, though it soon scrubbed clean, appeared as short as the day Hildebert had cropped it. While I now forgave her this crime, for it must have been trying indeed to dress such an uncooperative debutante, I mourned the loss of my long locks. Much as I disliked wigs, I might be forced to use them, for no amount of tonsorial genius could coax these strands into a pompadour—

A tremendous commotion broke my reverie as Beatrix and several other ladies in waiting burst into my bath.

"Oh, look at her!" said one of the ladies, peering into the tub. "'Tis a *miracle!*"

"Princess, you must stand and display yourself," pleaded Beatrix.

"I shall do no such thing! May I please have some privacy?"

Beatrix tossed me a dressing gown. "Don this—we will look away. Come, come, we must observe you!"

By the time I had robed, the small room was packed with ladies of the court marveling at my slim form, as they so described it flatteringly—and inaccurately, for I was by no possible stretch of the imagination slim. I was simply no longer rotund. Pleased as I had been to make this discovery about myself, I disdained the adulation of this flock of sharp-eyed gossips, for their tongues had stabbed me far too often in the past. I kept my silence as a modest young woman should. Nevertheless, inwardly I vowed never to debase myself with such superficiality. Without doubt a miracle had occurred, but my girth represented the least of it.

❀ ❀ ❀ ❀

The opportunity to display my new dedication to calling and country—for this be the miracle to which I allude—came about much earlier than I anticipated. In twos and threes, the twittering ladies drifted away, leaving Beatrix and Hildebert to review my wardrobe with unprecedented enthusiasm, given that I could now fit into the garments that had been prepared me.

"We shall dress you for dance class—if you feel quite up to it after your, ah, rest . . ." Lady Beatrix began. "If the queen has completed her matters of state by dinner, perhaps we can—"

At once a thought struck me—a true thought, and not simply an attempt at truancy. "What matters of state?"

"Oh, 'tis nothing to worry you."

"I am not so certain. Should not the nation's affairs concern the heir to the throne?"

Lady Beatrix twitched in surprise. "Well, I would not know—"

"I would like to believe that my best possible education this day would be to participate in whatever conference occupies the queen."

Too stunned to refute this logic, Lady Beatrix herself dressed and led me to the queen's salon, and nodded dumbly when I insisted the guard admit me.

The ex-salon doors opened to reveal Sophia and Lord Frederick in intense discussion with a stranger. At once my determination dissipated, and it was all I could manage not to retreat, knowing the verbal lashing to come.

And come it did. "What be the meaning of this impertinence?" demanded Sophia, fixing me with a glare.

"Forgive my presumption, Your Majesty . . . for too long I have avoided the affairs of Montagne. I must . . . I must commence to learn what I might." I gulped.

In the silence, I counted six ticks of the tall wall clock. Six seconds may not sound long, but at that moment they felt quite like eternity.

Lord Frederick spoke. "Your Majesty, it is a commendable goal. We can avoid discussing certain matters in her presence."

"Yes . . ." mused the queen. She nodded to an empty chair. "We admire your interest, Benevolence. This gentleman, so soon returned from Drachensbett, speaks to us of conditions in that nation."

"Ah, yes," said the stranger, struggling to maintain his composure in the wake of this drama. "I was just speaking of plans I'd heard, from a soldier come from a secret camp, to take the chateau from the mountain."

Relief flooded my bones! How extraordinarily fortuitous—now the castle could prepare for attack.

But to my horror, Sophia only waved him away. "Forever you hear this rumor, and forever we respond that such a feat is impossible. They would perish atop Ancienne! We are far more curious to learn of King Renaldo, and the counsel he seeks."

I knew I should hold my tongue—I had only been at the table a minute—but truly, every element of my position and my past demanded I speak. "If I may be so bold, Your Majesty—"

From around the room, I was examined with varying levels of outrage and disbelief.

Bravely I continued. "Perhaps this gentleman speaks true.

Do not forget that the murderers of King Ferdinand and my mother had to have crossed Ancienne."

Sophia regarded me icily. "Drachensbett denies any role in that tragedy."

"Nonetheless, I humbly suggest assembling a party of men skilled in the arts of mountaineering to ascertain once and for all the veracity of this gentleman's rumor."

Lord Frederick broke the ensuing silence. "It is a reasonable suggestion, Your Majesty. At worst, they would only deny his report."

I did my best to look demure, much as I wanted to bellow that I had seen this camp with my own eyes, that Drachensbett had of course killed King Ferdinand, and that anyone believing otherwise must be utterly deranged.

The queen, perhaps in her omniscience hearing my unspoken sentiments, in the end acceded. Talk shifted to management of the spring flooding, and then with a courteous tone I had never before heard—certainly not addressed to me—she asked that I depart so they might speak privately. Proud to my core of my new maturity, I withdrew.

I could not but wonder at the queen's unprecedented civility, until I realized with a flush of shame that it was my own improved behavior that motivated hers. So it is that we in life determine our own treatment.

❀ ❀ ❀ ❀

Trees along an ocean shore sway gently in the sun, heedless of the tidal wave that will soon sweep them away. So did these days pass as I busied myself, unaware of the deluge about to engulf Chateau de Montagne.

Monsieur Grosbouche near collapsed at my newfound dedication to my lessons. To my shock I now found dancing far from onerous. Indeed, I must confess that I learned the steps quite swiftly; perhaps my experience harrying his laces ultimately proved beneficial. Languages, penmanship, comportment . . . all I bore with enthusiasm. The only task I yet abhorred was needlework. Lady Beatrix, reluctant to remind me of Prince Florian's painful (so she thought) abandonment, no longer mentioned my need of tokens for admirers. Nonetheless, I was yet required to produce handkerchief after handkerchief in the manner of a mill grinding out flour. Sighing over my handiwork, she would urge me to take more care next time. I set to work anew, imagining each stabbing needle passing into Florian's scalp. (This may explain the poor quality of the resulting product.) I found energy even for table manners, reminding myself of the spitting, belching Drachensbett soldiers whenever the mincing fussiness of the royal table threatened my resolve. Several days following my revival, the castle celebrated my sixteenth birthday, the court marveling publicly, and me privately, at all that had transpired in the past year.

Then, after an absence of two weeks, the mountaineers returned. Guards along the ramparts cheered the appearance of the exhausted party—until the lieutenant, screaming from the drawbridge, demanded an immediate audience with the queen. His shout sent a spasm of fear through all who heard it, and trumpets raised to herald the soldiers' return sounded alarums instead.

The Privy Council convened hastily as the lieutenant, still in his mountain garb, paced the throne room. As the expedition had been initiated at my suggestion, Sophia graciously included me as well, and lost not a moment in encouraging the man to speak.

His shaggy face burnt with cold, the soldier described days clambering through boulders and snow, convinced of the foolishness of their assignment until a peculiar scar on a tree trunk, fresh enough yet to ooze sap, caught the eye of an attentive private. They then detected a second scar on a tree many paces up the hillside, and another. Following these blazes, the men found themselves climbing into the uncharted wilderness of Ancienne. Contrary to logic and expectation, their trek eased the farther they ascended, for whoever devised this route had located it along the most navigable terrain. They did not crest Ancienne until dusk, and the clear evidence of human footprints beneath the freshly fallen snow inspired them to pitch their tents in a hidden gully, and post guards throughout the night.

The next morning (the lieutenant continued), the Montagne scouts, weapons drawn, followed a trail now wide enough for four men to walk abreast. In only a day's trek they discovered a military camp, recently abandoned and with space enough for four hundred soldiers. The road from this camp, gouged with fresh hoof prints and sledge marks, led straight down the mountain to Drachensbett.

"We raced at once back to Montagne, delaying only to sleep and disguise our tracks. The trail, Your Highness, took us directly to the foundations of Chateau de Montagne." With this the lieutenant finished his recitation.

A murmur of horror rose as listeners realized how close

the nation had come to annihilation. Panicked whispers passed between brave and experienced men, and an elderly countess fainted.

Sophia lifted one hand into the air; the buzzing turmoil quieted. "We have underestimated the sagacity of our Benevolence."

"'Twas nothing, Your Highness," I blurted out, blushing in shame; brutal experience, not keenness of judgment, had led me to encourage the mountaineers' exploration.

"We must consider the situation. Though Renaldo now attempts a . . . a different scheme of conquest"—she avoided mention of the Claim of Benevolent Succession, as I was not supposed to know of it—"he will doubtless return to this mountain route should his stratagem fail. We must have maps at once, and engineers as well. Did you not hear us clearly?"

Footmen dashed off to scour the castle. Sophia sat as a statue, ignoring the attention upon her. Her poise alone, the flash of her eyes indicating great thought, allayed the panic that threatened to squeeze the air from the room.

At last engineers arrived, accompanied by a breathless geographer clutching a dozen maps, which he spread, with many apologies and calls for weights, before her.

Donning pince-nez, the queen scrutinized the documents, insisting that the lieutenant pencil his discoveries into the areas marked *uncharted wastes.* When at last she spoke, I jumped at the noise, for I had been quite mesmerized by the spectacle of the queen in spectacles.

"Come forward," she ordered the geographer. "Are we not correct in assuming that infiltrators must traverse this narrow canyon to reach our citadel? Pray answer honestly."

The man squirmed and perspired, but at last conceded the queen spoke true.

"Then we shall erect a barricade," proclaimed Sophia, her fingernail denting the paper, "precisely here. Just as that great work of the Chinese emperors preserved their nation from the Mongol hordes, so will this wall protect us. It shall be a marvel of construction, and it shall make our nation proud."

Sophia plunged into the construction of "Ferdinand's Wall" (as she christened it) with unprecedented and prodigious enthusiasm. Stating that she wished her husband's tomb completed for the country's biennial autumn festival, she assembled surveyors, miners, masons, bricklayers, blacksmiths, carpenters, charcoal burners, and myriad other laborers high up the mountain, sequestered from their families to put all their energy into the task. The ruse thus isolated the entire workforce from loose lips and spies. Claiming headache and the need for absolute solitude, she spent weeks at a time locked in her chambers—though in reality she, too, lived at the work site, sleeping each night in a small striped pavilion.

I had my own secret aspirations for Ferdinand's Wall. I longed to show my country my father's body and last words, his unequivocal indictment of Drachensbett, and to deliver him to my mother's side. Yet I could not reveal how I knew Prince Walter—King Walter—to be dead near the summit of Ancienne. Therefore, I prayed that the builders would somehow discover him, as his cave could not be more than half a day's climb from the Drachensbett trail. Alas, no Montagne explorer trekked that high, so cautious was every man about detection by Drachensbett. My father remained in his eternal sleep in that frigid cavern, frozen and alone. Disappointment, however, I kept to myself, and even heartbreak could not keep me from cheering the progress of this most essential fortification.

The construction had an even more profound effect on me than this, for Sophia, in setting herself the task of defending Montagne, promptly and remorselessly abandoned all her domestic duties. The countless decisions of Chateau de Montagne—the menus, the interminable cycle of cleaning, the food stores to be laid up for winter, the disciplining and acquisition of staff—now mattered to her not in the least, and to my astonishment I found myself time and again facing a petitioner in need of an immediate verdict, with no other authority to whom to turn.

My mistakes as de facto castle mistress were legion, and I shall not recount them here beyond offering the advice, well earned, that mint sauce should never be served with beef. But, having served as slave to the Drachensbett army, I reminded myself that other positions would surely be available should I fail as princess, and so set myself grimly to the task.

So quickly and profoundly did I transform from dour chrysalis to eager butterfly that the household whispered I must surely yet be enchanted. In response, the queen on one of her sporadic appearances declared that if this be enchantment, it was enchantment worth preserving, and any person breaking it would be punished most severely. This understandably cast a pall on my interactions with the staff. How I might have recovered from this unassisted, I know not. As it was, I stumbled quite by accident upon another undertaking that I am certain stunned not only the castle's occupants but the entire country.

It began one morning when Hildebert entered my chambers with a sneeze so loud that I feared her head would sail off her shoulders.

"Forgib be, Your Highness, it is nudding," she sniffled.

I begged to differ, and at once led her to the kitchens in my dressing gown—which set certain tongues wagging I am sure—and installed her in a staff parlor. I then assembled a tea of garlic, pepper, and gingerroot, the same concoction my mother had so often made me, and, carrying the redolent cup to her side, insisted she not leave her couch for the remainder of the day.

Strange as it may sound, the tea released fond and powerful memories of my mother—perhaps it was the smell, for we all of us have experienced that profound connection between scent and memory. I found myself again and again brewing another restorative draught for my handmaid. The power of rest being what it is, the woman healed quickly, with much praise for my care, and soon other staff members sought my advice for minor ailments—sore throats, stiff backs, an unfortunate boil. A baker with much hesitation and stumbling asked what I might recommend for his child suffering from stomachache. Scratching my head, I suggested a diet of peppermint tea and applesauce (another of my mother's remedies), and the baker returned the next week to inform me, awed, that it had worked to perfection.

I soon found on my rides through the valley—for I now insisted my equestrian lessons extend beyond the castle walls—that a farm wife would wave me down, or a small child in need of some attention for a family member would shyly catch my eye. I took to carrying a small pack on my pony's saddle for just such emergencies, though I included half the equipment only in my mother's memory, having no more notion how to use it than I would a blacksmith's anvil. But my modest efforts produced great results, for through my work I came to know and respect the people of Montagne, and they to know me as well. I do not presume to make assumptions of their *respect,* but they appeared to enjoy my company, and appreciate greatly my little therapies. When I presented a kitten to a suffering crone—for I suspected her aches stemmed primarily from loneliness—she threw her bony arms around me and with tears in her eyes announced that I could have no more suitable name in all the world than Benevolence. So it was that in aiding the residents of Montagne, I became acquainted most of all with my own dear mother.

❀ ❀ ❀ ❀

In those turbulent summer months I found serenity with two others as well. Curiously enough, it was Hildebert of all people who brought me peace with the first of these individuals. Strolling through Market Town with her one morning, I overheard a man and woman berating each other.

"How unhappy they sound!" I exclaimed. "Perhaps I could help."

"Nay, Your Highness, you'd best stay clear of those two. Some folks have pasts what prevent a future."

Her words, I reflected later, explained the relationship between my mother and the queen. That the two women had disliked each other was without question, and I admit my own hostility to Sophia stemmed in part from loyalty to Pence. As my opinion of the queen evolved, I often worried that in tolerating her I would somehow violate allegiance to my mother and her memory. Hildebert's wisdom thus reassured me mightily. Perhaps if my mother could see the queen now, attacking each construction challenge with the gusto of a sot uncorking a flagon, masonry dust caked to her skirts . . . But Pence was gone outside my memory, and I was left to chart my own future with the queen.

The second person with whom I made peace, my mother always in my consciousness, was none other than myself. When first I emerged from enchanted sleep, the castle population agreed that my newly reduced form would not last a month. As memories of Pence fed my heart, however, the hunger in my belly abated and I found that instead of comfort, I now ate for sustenance and, increasingly, taste (though my inroads on this front took far more time and diplomacy than I had anticipated). "Fill the stomach, not the soul," my mother used to say with a tweak of my nose as she watched me devour a fruit tart. Wise that she was, she recognized that for all the passion she put into her sauces and stews, food was only an emblem of devotion, not love itself. Now at last I saw the truth in her words.

I must clarify yet again that I was not willowy, slender, delicate, gauzy, diaphanous, fine-boned, or any of the other descriptives forever linked to the daughters of kings, and that my figure, however feminine, yet conveyed that I suffered little in cold draughts. The endless twaddle about my silhouette revolted me, and I grew ever more incensed over the general reliance on appearance alone for repute, rank, and virtue. I kept my ears pricked for any superficial judgment and would gently remind the speaker that the person of whom they spoke had many other qualities, good and poor, beyond complexion and waistline. This singular attempt to change the world's vanity took no small effort, but I derived great satisfaction from the measured conclusions the castle occupants eventually shared of each other—at least within my earshot.

❀ ❀ ❀ ❀

Given the activity that filled my days from dawn until long past nightfall, I had scant time for magical pursuits. When first I returned to Chateau de Montagne, I shied even from thinking the word *magic,* for I had no wish to rekindle the winter's hysteria. More than once I awoke in cold terror from a dream of Prince Florian announcing I was a witch. (Oddly, in the dream he murmured it fondly, stroking my hair as he leaned forward with a kiss.) Why he had not declared my status to all of Drachensbett, I could not deduce. In calmer moments I reminded myself 'twould be only his word against mine. Then, remembering his hissing disdain, I could not but believe that he found me too repellent even to discuss. The thought pained me, argue though I might that his opinion should not affect me in the least.

My feelings—about magic, not Florian—calmed with time, but still I avoided the Wizard Tower. Each night as I settled myself into bed, I would remember I had not visited my wizard room in some time and would promise to do so soon, perhaps the next day; at the moment, however, I coveted only sleep. And when the next day came, I was needed in so many places, not as a Doppelschläferin but as a thinking young woman, that again the promise slipped away. I had experienced enough magic for some time, and I was wise enough to sense that magic, like life, cannot be accomplished in bits and stolen moments but requires all of one's attention, and my attention, happily, was elsewhere.

SEVENTEEN

Drachensbett continued to press for an answer to their Claim of Benevolent Succession. Lord Frederick delayed and obfuscated, employing every weapon in his diplomatic arsenal. The queen's headaches, alas, prevented discussion. Then came rumor of Prince Walter, or a man much resembling Prince Walter, in far-off Farina. A party was dispatched at once to investigate. The man proved to be only a sailor fleeing debtors, with no relation to Prince Walter or our nation . . .

Summer passed; September bloomed. Diplomats, waiting in the throne room, demanded an answer. Hidden behind the throne room's portal, I chewed my knuckles in worry.

Choosing her words with utmost care, Sophia spoke. "We are most grateful for your concern for our country's welfare, and we have no wish to violate this most honored doctrine. Therefore, having no alternative, we honor your Claim of Benevolent Succession."

Her announcement sent a shock through the crowd—and Princess Benevolence.

"However . . . we make one small request. As you so clearly delineated when first you approached our court, the faults of the princess are legion. Yet of late she has applied herself with commendable diligence."

"Your Majesty—and I mean this as no insult to your efforts—I observed her with my own eyes," the ambassador uttered coldly.

"As have we all. But we, when our maladies permit, have also witnessed a transformation, and we cannot but believe, should the girl's enthusiasm continue, that she may yet develop—with proper mate, of course—into an acceptable ruler."

"The prince has no interest in her hand."

"That point has been made," the queen answered with equal frigidity. "Still, we would ask that Drachensbett for one month withhold its claim. October shall see our autumn festival, culminating with a great ball to honor our nation. At that event we shall present Benevolence to our neighbors, His Majesty Renaldo above all, that assessment of her capacity may be made."

Inside my secret passage, I near collapsed from panic.

The footmen nearest the portal peered about for the source of such peculiar squeaking until I gagged myself with my fist. Whose shoulders be broad and strong enough to bear the weight of a nation—to bear the weight when clad in an asphyxiating gown, trapped in the scorching beams of a thousand prying eyes? Not my shoulders, surely. Oh, if only the queen had asked me ere presenting me on a platter for the world to dissect! I could not imagine enduring a ball at all, particularly given the uniquely horrific circumstances of the previous one, and then to add to this toxic brew the requirement that I perform more admirably than ever a princess has, or my country be sacrificed forever . . .

Consulting with his group, the ambassador at last answered that he could not speak for his king and so must return to court for further instructions.

The queen nodded. Perhaps delay had been her intent all along, I thought with a leap of hope. The Drachensbett contingent withdrew, and, alone with my thoughts, I returned to my chambers and the nap upon which I had fervently insisted. That night at dinner, Beatrix and Sophia commented that my rest appeared to have left me oddly fatigued. As ever, no reference was made to Drachensbett, the queen not wishing to distress me.

❀ ❀ ❀ ❀

Days passed without answer. Eavesdropping, I learned that King Renaldo might easily construe Sophia's request as rejection, and so attack at his desire. The completion of Ferdinand's Wall grew ever more imperative, and bonfires burned through the night to light the men's work. The queen with her innate military instinct posted soldiers disguised as shepherds across Ancienne to detect any sign of infiltration. I could not but pity the soldiers, for the men came from shepherding stock, and grievous it must have been to return to the stinking flocks they had toiled so long to escape.

Then, a fortnight after that fateful meeting, these patrolling soldiers discovered two strangers wandering the upper reaches of Ancienne. Though the men appeared to be only travelers from faraway lands, the soldiers took no chances, and promptly escorted them to Chateau de Montagne. The queen insisted on questioning them herself, inviting Lord Frederick to participate and me to observe.

Led into the throne room, the men bowed in an adequate if generic fashion. They wore the dusty robes of wool merchants, down to the guild's rosette that guaranteed safe passage through foreign parts, and appeared suitably uncomfortable before the queen but not otherwise anxious.

"We have heard tales of the court of Montagne," the larger man spoke. "But we never imagined to one day behold its beauties."

"We appreciate your flattery," answered Sophia. "But still we wonder at your presence on our mountain, for its reaches are inaccessible to any but shepherd or sheep."

The man smiled. "That be the cause of our troubles. You see, my companion has heard talk of a rare goat, with wool akin to cashmere, that occupies Drach—ah, Ancienne, as you term it."

The queen stiffened at this mention of Drachensbett. "There is no goat."

The smaller of the men now spoke. "We know that now, all too well. But in our explorations—conducted, as you might appreciate, with great secrecy—we wandered farther than intended and so came to the attention of certain well-armed shepherds."

"Yes. Compelling your tale be. Yet our relationship with Drachensbett suffers, and should news of 'well-armed shepherds' reach their ears, it will not bode well." Though the queen's face remained impassive, I had spent enough time with the woman in recent months to develop some insight into her temper, and I could sense her burgeoning frustration.

"Your Majesty," I said softly. As one, the group turned upon me. Sophia frowned at my interruption, while the two strangers regarded me with the arrogance certain men forever display toward the weaker sex.

Only Lord Frederick supported me. "Yes, Your Highness?"

"May we present Benevolence, Crown Princess of Montagne," declared Sophia belatedly.

I swallowed. Since their entrance, I had studied the two men. Though their dress and mannerisms indicated without question their merchant status, I could not but wonder at their story. All my life I had devoured tales of Ancienne, more so since my return from Drachensbett, and now considered myself as well informed as the country's eldest sage. Yet never once had I heard whisper of cashmere goats. "Please, Your Majesty, their quest should be encouraged."

The two men beamed smugly as Sophia scowled. "Benevolence, you know not your place—"

"Do not forget that cashmere would line our pockets as well as their own. I suggest a platoon of soldiers accompany these merchants to the highest reaches of Ancienne, supply them with the most delectable foodstuffs—roast pig, spiced wine, hot meat pies—and, taking care to secure the merchants that they do not wander into the wrong hands, leave them for a week to conduct their investigation unimpeded."

The queen stared at me in shock, but I had eyes only for the strangers, whose erect confidence wilted with every word I spoke.

"D-de-delectable f-f-foodstuffs?" the smaller man asked. "S-s-secure?"

I nodded. "In a manner that would permit free movement about your campsite, of course. Perhaps some length of chain, a comfortable ankle ring?"

The men gaped in horror at each other. "That is—we would never want to disturb—we are not *ambitious* merchants—" the first man began.

"We are not merchants at all!" piped up the smaller one. He fell to his knees before the queen. Hastily the other followed, and together they reached for the queen's hem.

"Indeed," said the queen, flicking her skirt from their reach. "What be your work?"

"To m-monitor Montagne's activities, in pr-preparation for attack."

"Attack? When?"

The two men gulped, struggling for an answer.

"We quite relish," she prodded, "the notion of chaining you to Ancienne."

"They shall attack with the full moon! The prince leads a battalion to take the castle."

"Have you other information for us?"

"No. Truly! We were kept from further planning, lest we be . . . captured."

"The full moon comes tomorrow night," Lord Frederick whispered.

"Remove them!" Sophia gestured as if the two spies were overcooked beef. They were dragged from the room fearfully avoiding my eye.

Lord Frederick whooped and clapped me on the back with the enthusiasm of a man a third his age, and Sophia herself could not suppress a smile. "Tell us, Benevolence, how did you manage . . . We mean to say, how . . . ?"

"I simply presented to them the benefits of speaking the truth," I offered with a shrug.

"Yes, we recognize that! But why would Ancienne be viewed so fearfully?"

"I have heard talk"—I selected my words with care, for I

could not reveal too extensive a knowledge of our foe—"that the men of Drachensbett truly believe a dragon resides atop Ancienne. If the strangers hailed from that country, then this belief, I thought, might be used in our favor."

"And the roast pig?"

"In the stories I read as a child, dragons were forever lured to strong-smelling food."

The queen settled back with a satisfied smile. "Threatening them with a man-eating dragon . . . We must confess, Benevolence, that our esteem of you waxes with each passing day."

Aspire as I might to project queenly dignity, I could not restrain a flush of pride.

"Frederick, assemble a council of war that we might respond to the information our niece has so adroitly obtained."

* * * *

I had never expected that a war council would be so excruciatingly *dull.* Hours passed, twilight deepened, Venus twinkled through the window, stars one by one pricked the inking sky, and still they droned on about supply lines, revetments, chains of command, and optimal signal networks.

The entrance of Xavier the Younger brought new urgency to the proceedings. He had overseen every element of Ferdinand's Wall these past months, and he raced to join our council as soon as the messenger reached him. At once the queen questioned him on its completion.

"Another month, perhaps, Your Majesty," he said, shaking his head, "with men working 'round the clock . . . The two ends are done, mind you. It's the middle that's exposed."

"We do not have a month!" Sophia slapped the table. "We have a day! What of a temporary barricade?" Observing her, I recalled Prince Florian describing the woman as more general than queen. He had spoken critically, but at the moment I cherished her fierce determination.

"We've thrown one up, well as we can. But it won't survive flame or battering, I'll tell you that."

His voice faded as footsteps pounded in the corridor. Seconds later, a soldier burst into the room. "Flares—two flares! The attack has begun!"

"Are you quite certain?" the queen asked, her control calming the incipient panic.

"Yes, Your Majesty." The soldier nodded, panting. "Two flares—set off together—it has one meaning and one meaning only."

"They must have moved the attack forward when their spies did not return . . . Saddle our horse! Xavier? Frederick? We must depart at once!"

"Surely you don't mean *you're* going to battle?" Xavier interrupted.

"We most certainly are! This conflict requires our every attention."

"And mine!" I piped up, scurrying to fall in line behind her.

"You shall do no such thing!" Sophia roared, turning upon me.

"But I am heir to the throne—!"

"Yes! And as such, you shall remain locked in your chambers until your duties require you elsewhere. Frederick!" She paused and sighed, turning back to me. "Understand, Benevolence, that we . . . that should we . . . that you, my girl, represent Montagne . . . should we perish." And with a sweep of robes, she was gone.

* * * *

I pounded my bedroom door, raging and cursing, to no effect. How dare I be treated so! Once the queen had considered me worthless, and now apparently I was too valuable, but the end result was the same: dismissed while others conducted the affairs of state.

My fists began to complain of their pounding, and as I sank to the floor, my rational side pointed out that I had little to contribute to the field of battle. The army had healers enough, medics experienced in the treatment of war wounds. Nor, I suspected, did our soldiers require aid with their penmanship and table manners. Surely there was some role I could play in this hour of need, some element of my ridiculous education to put to use!

No, I realized with a start. Not *that* education. But the other one . . . I knew not how, exactly, but I could help. With trembling fingers I conjured a Doppelschläferin and dashed through the wall.

The wizard room was as I had left it, though dusty—remarkable, it is, how quickly dust gathers. Now arrived, panting from the climb, I had no further plan. The spell book lay closed on its pedestal; I would not receive guidance there. Nor had I use for that blasted magic looking glass. I peered about, desperate for some encouragement. The cabinets as always hovered in shadow, the wash bucket rested in one corner, the broom propped beside it—

Hair rose on my neck. The broom! I had left it shattered atop Ancienne! For it to have returned would be—

Its return would be magic. Unnerved though I was, I barked a laugh. A magic broom by definition surpasses reason. If it could fly, why not reincarnate? Who knew, indeed, of what the broom was capable? Steeling my heart, I reached out and felt that familiar tingle. Settling myself on the handle, I at once rose several inches into the air. Fly I could, that much was true. But what good would this do me, or my country? I needed to preserve my people, not provoke alarm.

Yet the broom had returned for some reason.

My hair brushing the ceiling timbers as the broom wandered, I pondered how I might possibly defend Montagne . . . At once the solution came to me, each component falling into place with wondrous clarity. My feet thudded to the floor. Grasping the broom, I raced downstairs, past the portal to my cell, farther downward, and, pausing only to clarify that I was alone, into the queen's privy chambers. Through the reception area I dashed, through the bedroom, the bath, a parlor, finally locating her dressing room.

Mirrored wardrobes lined the walls; padded brackets displayed hats, caps, veils, and bonnets. I flung open one door after another, attempting even in my madness to preserve the neat piles, for my disheveling would only cause another's punishment. At last, buried at the bottom of a trunk, I found it: a gown of poppy red silk laced with gold. Spreading it before me now, I marveled anew at fate. Had the queen, so clothed in this serpentine fabric, not lashed my palms that momentous evening, I might never have discovered the magic portal. I would not be here at this moment, exuberantly donning a dress I once abhorred. The high neckline, the train that extended a body length or more behind me . . . though the bodice drooped and puckered, and I tripped over the hem, the effect would not be altogether wide of the mark.

Admiring myself in the mirror, I caught sight of a most remarkable headdress of netting and golden horns (or so it appeared, unschooled as I am in the millinery arts), and I attached it to my head at once. Grasping my broom—but no, that would not do: the broom must at all costs remain hidden!—I lifted my skirts, and with no minor embarrassment worked the broomstick under the gown's waistband to my bosom. Leaning forward, my hands awkwardly clasped to my chest, I rose into the air and flew so hastily to the window that I quite smacked my forehead against it. The latch unlocked, the frame swung open, and I was in flight, the long train flapping and snapping behind me.

❀ ❀ ❀ ❀

The precipice from which Chateau de Montagne rises is not a cliff in its own right, but rather a diminutive extension of the north face of Ancienne. The queen's dressing room overlooked this precipice, and thus I providentially found myself but a moment's ride from the protection of Ancienne herself. So long as I hugged this cliff face I could avoid detection, for I had no desire to feel the sting of my own country's arrows, particularly when the broom required all my attention.

My last airborne experience, I now recalled grimly as I reeled and plunged, had not been the most elegant demonstration of enchanted flight, and though my life at the moment was not nearly so threatened, I had little time to waste mastering navigation. Focusing on the first star that caught my eye, I ascended until I convinced myself that even the most owl-eyed soldier could not discern me. Lurching, I rose over the cliff's edge. Below me, farmhouse lights twinkled, scattered across the valley, and a line of torches bobbed and shimmered against the flank of Ancienne.

My heart dropped—and my body as well, until I refocused—for those torches belonged to none other than Sophia and her retinue en route to the battlefield. As I continued to climb, I could now perceive bonfires at Ferdinand's Wall, and the Drachensbett army crawling down the mountainside as molten rock oozes from a belching volcano.

My grandfather had died battling Drachensbett. My uncle had been slaughtered defending my mother from that insidious nation. My father perished tracking those killers to their dank home. Montagne's time had come at last.

So swiftly did I fly that the wind brought tears to my eyes, and snatched them away. Soon enough the canyon spread beneath me, and like Jove himself I could observe the forces at work. The Drachensbett army had downed a massive tree—a Montagne tree!—and even now soldiers pounded it against the barricade that Montagne had desperately erected. Ever more Drachensbett men poured into the canyon, gathering around great bonfires as their archers traded shots with the defenders. Once the battering ram completed its dreadful work—and even at my great height I could hear the repeated thud, a veritable metronome of death—Drachensbett soldiers would pour through the gap, overwhelm the defenders, and proceed down the mountain.

Xavier's presence, the queen's, were immaterial; defeat would come regardless.

But not mine, I thought grimly. The battering ram I could not stop, but perhaps I could cast fear into the hearts of its operators. With a roar, I plunged through the air toward the wall. The red silk train streamed and snapped behind me—I prayed the fabric would hold against the strain—and as I drew closer, I released my hold on the broomstick, clutching it solely with legs and gown.

A great shout broke out! The men wielding the battering ram gawked so that I gazed into a score of open mouths. Muttering the spells for fire and wind, I shot a great flame at their heads.

I had anticipated reaction, yes, and hoped for fear—I had dressed as a dragon, after all, to the best of my abilities—but I had not foreseen defiance. The Drachensbett archers, far from treating my appearance as warning, appeared to consider me as a most entertaining target. As I banked skyward, countless arrows whistled past. Panicked, I sped faster, and perhaps this changing velocity prevented the archers' success. I did not at the time have the luxury to analyze.

Again I hovered far above the battle scene, my sweaty hands clenching the broomstick through the silk. I dared not attempt another pass. Already the attackers strove to lift the great log—they had dropped it in their astonishment, which offered me some solace—as hundreds of men scanned the heavens.

And then, I saw him. In a ring of torchlight, sword slashing the air, he issued commands from astride his stallion. Even from afar I recognized the gleam of silver crown, the undivided attention that every man in his earshot proffered and he without acknowledgment received.

Oh, how I despised Prince Florian! As an arrow is shot from a crossbow, so did I launch myself at him now. Defense mattered, yes, but I lusted for vengeance, the retribution a woman must exact from the man who has insulted her past all endurance. Again a shout rose—I had been spotted, but I cared not. Florian craned upward, his mouth ajar. Screaming the spell to the winds, I formed a rock and with all my might hurled it at that perfect head.

For the first, and perhaps the only, time in my life, my missile met its target. Alas, the quality of the spell did not equal my aim. Instead of granite or razor-sharp obsidian, I had created . . . mud. I craved the crack of stone against skull, perhaps even a crash as Florian collapsed from his horse. Instead, as I rose through the air, another volley of arrows singing past my ears, I heard only a wet smack followed by a yelp of surprise. And then—I was hit!

I lurched and spun as Drachensbett soldiers cheered. Glad I was to hold the broom inside my gown, or the force of impact would have thrown me off. Still I managed to rise through the arrows' onslaught, their volume lessening as I ascended. When the bonfires below appeared no more than coals, I slowed. Fearfully I felt about my body. My fingers found a shaft. I tugged, wincing in anticipation, but felt no pain. Encouraged, I yanked hard and found myself grasping an arrow, its head untouched by blood. Sophia's gown, I realized with a snort of relief, had so many layers that the arrow was halted ere it reached my skin.

With a rude curse I had learned in Drachensbett, I tossed the arrow back at my enemies. It glided down, turning end over end. I could not even *drop* something properly. At once, my martial spirit vanished completely. Enthusiasm, revenge: gone. My one conceivable contribution to the protection of my nation had failed. My damaged right arm throbbed from the demands of my spell work. Fatigue flooded my veins. The lights of Chateau de Montagne at this moment appeared as distant as the stars themselves. My shoulders sagged, my head drooped forward in utter exhaustion. The broom, devoid of guidance, spiraled downward into the wilds of Ancienne as darkness pressed against my closed eyes, swallowing my consciousness. I knew no more.

EIGHTEEN

MY EYES FLUTTERED OPEN. I was in a bed, my bed, in my own Peach Rooms. How had this possibly transpired? Yet before I could gather my wits, Prince Florian appeared chuckling in the doorway. He grinned, shaking his head. "You thought you'd bested me!"

Caught in his gaze, I could not turn away. He stepped closer, and with a warm hand stroked my cheek. He leaned toward me: "Will you never learn the truth?" His soft whisper tickled my ear, and I felt his breath as his lips drew closer—

"You'd sleep the entire day away if I let you."

My eyes flew open. Looming over me was the wide, florid face of Hildebert.

I jerked upright, gasping for breath. Sunlight poured through the bedroom windows, illuminating the rosebud duvet beneath which I lay.

"The entire castle's abustle," Hildebert sniffed, "and you dally as if naught in the world was amiss."

Frantically I scrubbed at my face—the sensation felt tangible enough, and painful. This was not a dream, not anymore. "What—who—how did I get here?"

"From the belly of a woman as all folk do. Now rouse yourself, did not you hear me? The queen wants to see you."

Aching and creaky, memories of the night's adventures pummeling my wits, I consented to Hildebert's ministrations. I had no memory of my return to the castle, and indeed have none to this day. Whether it be magic or amnesia I cannot say, but rest assured the experience was altogether unnerving, particularly when compounded by yet another nightmare about Florian. And—most important!—what of the battle?

"Quit sputtering—and what have you done to yourself now?" she snorted, pointing to an enormous purple bruise that covered fully half my bottom.

'Twas miracle indeed I had survived that Drachensbett arrow. Perhaps the bulk of fashionable skirts served more purpose than I realized. "I . . . must have stumbled."

"You're the soul of grace, you are. Get this on now before they come calling again." And she would say no more as she hurried me into my clothes, eliciting a yelp or two as she caught my bruise, and trotted me out of my chambers.

❊ ❊ ❊ ❊

I was escorted to the Hall of Flags. The battle, then, could not have been complete defeat, for the room honored the nation's greatest victories. There I found the queen and Frederick, their clothes yet soiled from travel, in a crowd of courtiers and common soldiers. Popping corks greeted my entry, though the festive mood could not overcome the fright this noise gave everyone, myself included.

The queen, haggard from lack of sleep, beamed at me. "Benevolence! You appear no more rested than we, dear child."

I gulped. "I spent much of the night fearing for my country. I beg you, please, what happened?"

"It is a marvelous tale, truly marvelous . . . Has everyone a glass? Then we propose a toast: To the Drachensbett dragon!"

Drinking deep, the others paid little heed to my choking response to these words, though a footman pounded me on the back with advice to hold off on champagne 'til I be older. More champagne flowed, and with many interruptions and clarifications, the weary but ebullient soldiers described the night's battle.

Forewarned, the Montagne forces had spent the afternoon securing the fortification, and so had some defense ready when the soldier shepherds high up Ancienne sent word of the approaching army. Indeed, these shepherds preserved Montagne as well as anyone, for they drove their flocks across the narrow Drachensbett trail, obliging the attacking forces to brake their advance, for as everyone knows, sheep in panic take direction from no one. When at last the army reached the canyon, Prince Florian's men wasted no time in felling a battering ram while officers readied their troops to pour through the pending gap. Gallantly Montagne's soldiers struggled to maintain the barricade, but the relentless hammering shattered plank and stone.

I nigh chewed off my tongue. *What of the dragon?* I longed to scream. Nor could I sit—the Drachensbett arrow had seen to that—but could only pace in the manner of Sophia herself.

At last the soldiers came to the heart of the story: without warning, a red dragon plunged from the sky, spewing flame at the battering ram.

"Smaller it was than I'd imagined a dragon to be," offered one of the men.

"And it shrieked right like a girl," another said, his companions nodding in agreement.

I turned to hide my blush, but I might as well have stood behind a magic portal, so little attention did I receive. The others had eyes only for the soldiers.

The Drachensbett forces were understandably stunned by this turn of events, and while some soldiers shot at the creature, others screamed to hold fire against the symbol of their nation at long last come to life. Enthusiasm vanished completely when the dragon reappeared, streaking straight toward Prince Florian.

"The prince sat there froze as a block of ice. And then just when you'd think the dragon would burn him, or gobble him up, the beast does just the opposite." The soldier paused, struggling for words. His companions squirmed in embarrassment.

"Yes?" prodded the queen.

"He, well—the beast, I mean—he, you know, *relieved* himself. Right on the prince."

Sophia reddened as a titter spread through the hall, and the soldiers did their best not to snicker. "'Prince Chamber Pot' he'll be called from now on, I reckon," one of the soldiers offered. "You can imagine what this did to his men, seeing their leader treated so by their own special critter. That was an omen, all right." The others agreed, and related how the attackers, taking their wounded with them, began an immediate retreat up the mountain.

"In no time at all, you couldn't see naught but the battering ram left behind, and their fires."

"Couldn't even see the dragon's you know what. It was all mixed with the mud and such."

The soldiers trailed off, their last words echoing in the silent hall as listeners struggled to absorb this extraordinary news. As amazement succumbed to exuberance, the room at once burst into chatter and cheers.

"What a miraculous tale!" one of the ministers exclaimed. "We must ring the church bells! Announce it to the land!"

"No!" the queen barked. "Absolutely not." She scowled at the gathering before her. "Do you not see? Should word of this humiliation reach the world, Renaldo will have no choice but to attack us once more in order to salvage his honor, and that of his son. Our country is far better served remaining silent." She studied the room and waited until she had the reluctant concurrence of every listener. "Soldiers, do you understand? It shall be your task to enforce this, and on pain of death you shall do so." She softened. "This does not mean you cannot celebrate amongst yourselves, for the victory is not solely due to dragons." With a nod, she dismissed them, and the rest of the gathering as well.

I turned to depart, for I needed time alone to absorb this information. Was it possible that I had saved Montagne? I staggered at the thought.

"Benevolence? We would you remained at our side a moment longer." Reluctantly I joined the queen strolling beneath the flags. "A most remarkable turn of events, is it not? To think that dragons actually exist!"

"Yes . . ."

She clasped my hand. "This glorious news removes a great weight from our heart, and yours as well, we are sure."

"Your Majesty, I am not certain I know of what you speak."

"Why, Benevolence, Drachensbett spoke true! Our husband and your mother were not the target of assassins after all. They were killed by that most dreadful beast."

In shock, I withdrew my hand from the queen's. "That had not occurred to me."

"Imagine—our beloved husband, slain by a dragon . . . Much as we yet mourn him, 'tis a fittingly *honorable* death, do not you think?"

I fought back tears. "Your Majesty, it is not . . . That is to say—"

She paid my devastation no heed. "Now at last we may normalize relations between our two nations. We have much work to prepare for this ball, dear girl, for we now have ever more reason to celebrate."

Once again, Sophia's keen political instinct proved true. When the Drachensbett ambassadors reappeared at our gates some days later, they made not one mention of the ill-fated battle on the slopes of Ancienne. After giving the matter great consideration, they explained, the king now agreed that Princess Benevolence should be afforded the opportunity of proving herself at the autumn ball ere he proffered his Claim of Benevolent Succession.

The Montagne listeners accepted this speech without a single whisper or sidelong smirk. Regally, the queen thanked Drachensbett for their patience and promised that both ball and princess would reflect well upon the kingdom of Montagne.

The weeks leading up to the ball I spent in an anxious daze as I pondered the crisis I had inadvertently brought upon my country. The people of Montagne now accepted without question that a vicious dragon was behind the Badger Tragedy. Not a soul would support my testimony, should I have had courage or madness to express it, that my mother and uncle and father had been killed by cold-blooded men whose plotting maneuvers would never end. When I attempted to broach the subject, however delicately, with the queen, she dismissed it with a wave and expressed again her hopes that relations between our two countries might now normalize.

The autumn festival arrived, with feasting, beer gardens, dances and plays, the judging of livestock, and of course the dedication of my uncle and mother's tombs beside the Badger's. I participated in these events as well as I could manage, though always our enemy occupied my consciousness.

At last came the day of the ball, cloudless and perfect. I joined queen and court as they readied themselves to usher Drachensbett's visitors to Chateau de Montagne. Our escort party made a most wondrous spectacle: a squad of soldiers in polished armor, their tabards embroidered with the golden hedgehog; the lords of the court, and some ladies as well, in their riding best; and at the forefront Sophia and I perched sidesaddle on gleaming mares. (Alas, my own sturdy mountain pony had been replaced this day by a horse that would bring me to eye level with our guests.) The crowds of Market Town cheered as we passed, and vivid banners snapped against the autumn sky.

"You ride well, Benevolence," murmured Sophia.

"Thank you, Your Majesty."

"We would that you accompanied King Renaldo to the castle," she continued, without a change to her expression, as she waved to the crowd.

I did my best to match her polished air, though horror clenched my heart. "If it pleases Your Majesty, I would serve better remaining in the background."

"Quite the opposite. You must demonstrate your admirable competence."

"But I have no competence! That is, in situations such as this—"

Sophia sniffed. "Young people forever believe that kingdoms are made on the field of battle. Believe me, dear princess, they survive or perish not through warfare but through gestures and dances and incidental conversations. As you desire the preservation of your country, you must act on this reality. Behold, our guests await us!" Her counsel given, she trotted toward the red dragon flag snapping above Drachensbett's elite.

If ever I required the charms of a princess, now would be the moment.

As a herald announced the guests, I could not resist a glance at Prince Florian, who sat rigidly astride his mount, ignoring me with every vibrating fiber of his being. King Renaldo was no more enthusiastic, barely responding to our introduction as the queen abandoned me to my fate.

Renaldo knew me only from the disastrous winter ball. Nothing he had heard since—not from his advisors, and certainly not from his son—would give him a single reason to believe me improved. Worse still, on his edgy stallion he loomed a head or more above me.

"A lovely day, is it not?" I gulped.

He grunted.

"And the castle presents such a lovely spectacle from this viewpoint. Do you not agree?"

"Most impressive," the king said, looking away.

"Indeed, when I was a girl I dreamt of creating a cake in its exact likeness. I would have used raspberries for the battlements, and bits of chocolate for the windows, and, I do not know . . ." I made a little frown as my mind raced, for I was fabricating this story as I spoke and had not a clue whereto it led. "Perhaps a lovely red apple for each tower."

"Wouldn't work," the king snorted.

"How splendid that you know this! Have you assembled such a cake yourself?"

"Hmph. Raspberries aren't in season with apples."

"Oh. That is such a clever point, I would never have thought it. What fruit, pray tell, would be appropriate with raspberries, for they are my favorite part of summer?"

"Well. Strawberries, if you banked them. Grapes—I don't think so, not yet. Perhaps string beans . . ."

"Beans! How fanciful. Who would have thought to make a castle of beans. Tell me, Your Majesty, how in all your duties have you become so knowledgeable about these humble plants?"

The king stiffened. "Humble, you say? These plants be our survival! Are you aware that my country produces four varieties of nectarine?"

And so as I rode toward Market Town was I lectured on

the timing of pruning, the necessity of trellises, the value of banking (by which, I gathered, he meant soil rather than gold), and the damage wrought by boring worms. Information verily poured from his lips, and when at last he made a small but honorable witticism on the crafting of grafting, I laughed out loud in relief.

The king glanced at me. "You sound like Pence."

His comment brought me up short. "I—I did not realize you knew my mother."

"We'd speak at state functions. A good woman. Excellent knowledge of herbs."

At this moment we entered the crowds of Market Town, providing me time to collect my thoughts. What would compel him to mention my mother, particularly given his role in her death?

With great effort I composed myself. "I should relish someday examining *your* gardens, Your Majesty."

"I freely admit they are quite pleasing, arranged following the plans of a most esteemed gardener to the king of France. Perhaps you have heard of him . . ."

Prince Florian rode past my other side, jeering a word in my ear.

Shocked, I spun about, but already his back was to me.

"My son is very handsome," King Renaldo pointed out, misinterpreting my action.

I struggled to regain my composure. "That he is, though surely I am too inexperienced to speak of such matters."

As courtesy dictates, the king offered a flattering response, but I heard naught. All I could dwell upon was Prince Florian, the antagonism that radiated like heat from his body, and the word he had spat under his breath in my direction: *witch.*

❀ ❀ ❀ ❀

My duties notwithstanding, I demanded a nap that afternoon, for my conversation with Renaldo had drained me completely. Sophia consented, for she was greatly pleased with my efforts, and praised me effusively ere I retired.

I must have slept, for soon dusk hovered outside my window, and Hildebert rustled about, eager to dress me. What a contrast to my last ball! Now I easily consented to the layers in which I was encased, and the efforts of a hairdresser to turn my locks, with many pins and hidden poufs, into a presentable entity. My gown suited me as well as I could ever hope, though I could not but envy the young ladies who would attract the honest compliments of the night. My bodice did not plunge as dramatically as some, and no man—no man I would ever want to meet, surely—could fit his hands round my waist. But the gown had the simple elegance for which Queen Sophia's dressmaker was so renowned, and what I lacked in beauty I would simply have to earn with charm. Donning the high-heeled slippers that would bring me more or less to the height of my guests, I departed my chambers.

The ballroom glowed with a thousand candles, the chandeliers glittered with a thousand shimmering rainbows, the banquet tables groaned beneath a thousand delectable dishes. I took Lord Frederick's arm at the top of the stairs, and careful I was to assist him, for the gentle old man was ever frailer.

Across the ballroom, chatter faded at the announcement of my name, and every eye watched my descent. "Well done, Ben," Lord Frederick murmured as we reached the parquet at last. "Your beauty has attracted quite a swarm."

So utterly had I focused on navigating the steps that I overlooked the crowd. Now I could see all too clearly a half-dozen peacocks—or drones, as Lord Frederick better described them—striving to make their introductions. First in line, to my disbelief, was none other than King Renaldo.

He bowed. "My lord, if you may be persuaded to part with her, I should greatly appreciate the company of Her Highness."

"The princess must of course share the first dance with our most esteemed neighbor," Lord Frederick answered smoothly.

Across the room, Sophia observed me closely; if nothing else, I must not fail her. Suppressing a grimace, I assembled my questions, formulated this afternoon, on the cultivation of fruit trees.

The king led me to the center of the dance floor. He bowed, I curtsied, we danced.

"Sophia is a most handsome and capable woman," Renaldo commenced.

"Indeed, she has every possible attribute a woman of her position could require."

"And several more. She is, I have heard, quite adept at military architecture."

This parry caught me quite by surprise, and for a moment I could only laugh. "Is not the fairer sex best equipped to generate the harmonious union of esthetics and practicality?" I considered this response quite brilliant, particularly as it neither confirmed nor denied his statement.

"So, you believe fortifications to have an inherent beauty?"

"Certainly—when they succeed." I paused long enough for this jab to sink in. "Of course, even their failure would not faze our queen. Were the castle under attack and without defenders, she would yet stand on the ramparts launching arrows at her foes."

"And you, Princess, where might you be found? In your chambers, attending to your embroidery?"

"Oh, I have no skill whatsoever with a needle! No, without a doubt you would find me at her side, boiling oil." I smiled, revealing the teeth behind my lips. "But such talk of warfare has no place here. Tell me, Your Majesty, do you happen to know if a plum when intended to become a prune is left on the vine or plucked ripe?"

The king studied me. "You know already that a plum does not grow on a vine."

"If I revealed that truth," I responded, laughing, "then we should have nothing to discuss."

We danced in silence for some time. "I must confess," murmured the king, "that I arrived at Chateau de Montagne with a far different image of Princess Benevolence than what you present this evening."

"I shall forgive such a dreadful transgression only if the new image be more flattering." (Good heavens, I was turning into a most dreadful flirt!)

"You can be certain I would not have spoken otherwise." He frowned over my shoulder. As we turned, I caught sight of Florian dancing enthusiastically with a beautiful young lady whose bosom, I must say, remained in its encasement through goodwill alone. The prince could not have snubbed me more completely.

King Renaldo scowled. "Forgive my son, Princess, for not paying you the attention you deserve."

"Think nothing of it. How could a man surrounded by such roses note a simple fleur-de-blanc?" (here naming a diminutive local flower).

"With maturity, a man realizes that the quality of a bloom matters far more than its boast."

At this, the dance ended and with thanks for his company I departed the king's side, my head quite spinning from the nuances of our conversation and from my fear that I had unwittingly misspoken.

For the rest of the night I danced with every able man in the room save Prince Florian. King Renaldo requested my hand twice more. Several times I noticed him lecturing Florian, or so it appeared from the resentment with which the prince accepted his words, and the prince's attitude grew ever frostier as the night progressed.

With time my toes began to throb in their little prisons and I depleted completely my store of innocuous and winning pleasantries. Were it not for the invigorating qualities of champagne and the many compliments I was paid, I would have not survived at all. In her omniscience, the queen sensed my exhaustion and, recognizing that fruit is best picked ripe, released me as the clock struck midnight. Lord Frederick escorted me from the room, heaping praise on my weary frame.

We had scarcely progressed past the ex-ballroom, however, when sharp footsteps and a sharper "Your pardon, sir" brought us up short.

Prince Florian addressed Lord Frederick. "If I might have a moment of the princess's time."

Seeing my nod, Frederick stepped away to examine a tapestry.

"Your Highness," I greeted him, matching his chill.

Florian paced, too angry to meet my eye.

My feet ached, my very bones drooped with exhaustion. "If you carry a message of substance, I shall receive it; otherwise these pleasantries can surely wait for morn."

"Your behavior is despicable!" the prince snapped.

"In what way?" I snapped back. "You have no cause to criticize me."

"No cause? I vowed, the moment I left that cursed Blue Room and your conniving sorcery, never to speak of what I had witnessed, and until this day I had no incentive to do so. Since our arrival in this demon castle, however, as I witness your handiwork, I cannot but fear for the preservation of all that I hold dear."

"My handiwork? As hostess and emissary?"

"Emissary? Hostess? Do not toy with me! I am no longer some innocent trapped by your lies and spell work! I demand, should you value your life and the lives of your people, to break at once the enchantment you have placed upon my father!"

So staggered was I by this fallacious and spiteful accusation that I nigh broke my ankle on the ridiculous heels on which I tottered. "Enchantment, you say? It is enchantment to practice dance for hour after hour, day after day, with a man who reeks of fish? To ride, and write, and prattle incessantly about nothing whatsoever? To stitch enough handkerchiefs to dam the Great River itself, and bully one's body into clothes more suitable for martyrs than ladies?" I snatched up one of my cursed slippers. "Does this smack of magic to you? Because allow me to inform you, my handsome young prince, that this be not enchantment—it be work!"

With that, I hurled the slipper at him, not caring if I caused his decapitation. (I did not.) Marshaling what little dignity I yet possessed, I stomped down the corridor—challenging indeed with one shoe—and around the corner.

I lay awake for hours. The prince had no right, not one, to indict me so, and if I had held the slightest hope of the book's assistance, I would have climbed at once to my wizard room for a spell with which to punish him. Death, perhaps, or humiliation. A croaking frog would be nice, particularly a frog that retained Florian's dark eyes. I should keep it in a box and poke it occasionally with a stick; that would be satisfying indeed.

Calming myself in degrees with such pleasant notions, I drifted at last to sleep.

NINETEEN

I BREAKFASTED IN MY CHAMBERS, occupying myself with reports from the staff. A stolen pearl necklace demanded much of my attention until the crisis was finally resolved by a diligent manservant who discovered it in a potted palm, discarded there by an inebriated duchess.

When at last I appeared at the luncheon buffet, I was stunned to see Prince Florian glowering down at his plate. I had quite expected him to vacate the castle at the first light of dawn. Beside him, King Renaldo rose at once to inquire on the quality of my rest. Both father and son appeared fatigued, though I had no place to criticize, given my own countenance.

Chatting with our other guests, I paid the two little mind until Renaldo, sidling up beside me, requested a word with the queen.

I shuddered. Florian must have told him of my sorcery—

doubtless with horrific embellishments. I attempted a delay, to no avail.

"Please, Princess, it is of no small importance to me."

Thus in due time he, Sophia, and I gathered in the very Blue Room in which Florian half a year earlier had so unsuccessfully tried to revive me. Renaldo perched on his chair, wringing his hands, and I suppressed the urge to do the same. Perhaps I might yet deny witchcraft, or swear it off, should the queen appear sympathetic to this tack.

"Your Majesty," Sophia began. "Please share with us the cause of your anxiety that we might offer succor."

"It is difficult to discuss." The king winced.

"If there be any misunderstanding, we pray you accept our apologies."

"Nay, you are both the embodiment of hospitality . . . Your Majesty, Your Highness, I ask leave only—might I this afternoon visit Ferdinand's tomb?"

Inevitably, Sophia recovered first from this thunderbolt. She insisted even that I escort him, as she had obligations with our other guests.

No task ever attracted me less. I found the king's solicitude as disturbing as his earlier disdain. The thought even crossed my mind that he might be luring me to my mother's fate. Yet no matter how strongly I pleaded, Sophia would not relent. "Courtesy is our weapon of choice at the moment, dear Benevolence, and the one wielded best."

My heart sank still further, be that possible, when the king arrived accompanied by Florian, though I could not say whether the prince or I appeared the more reluctant. Renaldo, for his part, lost in his own thoughts on his skittish mount, so hurried to reach the tomb that he paid his son no heed whatsoever, providing the two of us far too much opportunity to expand on the conversation that had so dramatically finalized my departure from the ball.

"How delightful the pleasure of your company on our outing," I began, using a tone I had learned from Sophia.

"I cannot claim credit for this promotion," he replied, staring straight ahead.

"Indeed you cannot. But you are a most loyal son."

"I endeavor always to protect my father."

"You yet accuse me of enchantment?"

"It is dragons on broomsticks I fear most," he answered coldly.

This counter verily struck the breath from my body.

"You do not deny it," he spat out. "I knew I was correct. But what is one voice of reason in a multitude clamoring of 'dragons'? Particularly when that one voice has been silenced by the most profound dishonor?"

"'Tis dishonor to lose a battle? Accept it, dear prince; it is an incontrovertible fact—"

"Prince Chamber Pot," Florian hissed.

My ears burnt in shame; I could not prevent it. "I did not do that—"

"You did not?" Florian's voice shook with fury. "You did not set out to humiliate me in the most calculating, vicious, unforgettable—?"

"I was attempting to protect my country!"

"By besmirching my life?" He spurred his horse forward, away from my side.

Oh! That the prince should believe me capable of *splattering* him, as though I had ever once performed such calculated vulgarity . . . He did not deserve to be a frog. Not even a toadstool.

At last our party arrived at the glade that held the final resting place, so recently dedicated, of the king and my mother. Sunlight glittered on the Ancienne stone, the mountain's peak high above us.

King Renaldo dismounted as if sleepwalking and stumbled to Ferdinand's tomb, running his hand over its surface.

For a moment I felt a pang of regret that Prince Florian and I abhorred each other so, for dearly would I have loved to exchange an eyebrow at this eccentricity.

"Florrie, come here," the king ordered.

Flushing at his childhood nickname, the prince did so.

"Touch this."

Florian complied, his stance revealing his mortification that I of all people should witness this.

"What does it feel like?" the king asked.

"It feels like rock, Father," the prince answered.

"Yes, but is it . . . What temperature is the rock?"

"It is *rock* temperature. It feels like the day. Like the air."

"Like the *air?*" the king probed. "It does not feel cold?"

Florian shook his head, as baffled as I over his father's performance.

The king's shoulders fell. "I should have known . . . It is of no mind. Let us return to the castle. Blitzen!" He snapped for his stallion.

"Father . . ." Florian glanced uneasily in my direction but could not contain his curiosity. "Pray tell, what be the meaning of all this?"

"'Tis only a dream I had, a ridiculous dream. Last night."

"Please, Your Highness," I interjected, "I should very

much like to know it, for memorable it must have been to bring us to this place."

The king sighed. "Memorable, yes, but of no import. I was abed—in this dream—and through the open window drifted a specter that uttered words I cannot forget. At once I awoke, my room empty and the window sealed. Doubtless it was the wine, or the disturbed sleep that often accompanies a strange environment—though fret not, Princess, for the chamber is most comfortable."

"What did it say, Father?" asked his son.

Renaldo gathered his reins, preparing to mount. "It said—now, let me recite this correctly—it said, 'The last Montagne ruler lies frozen in a tomb of ice, and only the next can find him.'"

"A tomb of ice!" Florian laughed. "'Tis a glorious autumn day—'twould be impossible! That tomb is warm as a bed. You felt it yourself—"

The sky whirled about my head. I clutched at my pony's mane.

The king stepped toward me. "Princess, are you quite all right?"

"Say it again," I whispered.

"The words? 'The last Montagne ruler lies frozen in a

tomb of ice, and only the next can find him.' Does this have meaning for you?"

"My father—" I swallowed. "My father lies in a tomb of ice."

"But that is imposs—Do you know this? Do you know where?"

My eyes looked to the snow-clad peak of Ancienne. When I turned back, the king was locked in a wordless conversation with Florian.

At this moment a horrible scream reached our ears: a man, somewhere on the slopes above us, in the throes of agony. The king's stallion started, then bolted at once down the path.

"What was that?" Renaldo exclaimed.

"I do not know, but someone is hurt desperately," I answered, and with no thought but to that of rescue, I dug my heels into my pony's flanks and raced up the mountain.

❀ ❀ ❀ ❀

I followed the path to Ferdinand's Wall, assuming as I did that the cries came from a laborer injured there. The next scream, however, proved me wrong, for it emanated from a different slope altogether. At once I turned my pony in this new direction, beating toward the sufferer through the brush, the terrain untouched by the boot of man. Another scream rent the air, echoing down the hillside. A great crash—and Prince Florian broke through the scrub behind me.

"What do you think you're doing?" I snapped, incensed with myself for my fright, and with him for many reasons.

"A prince always rides to the aid of a lady," he answered stiffly.

"Ha! Your father forced you to this."

His silence confirmed my accusation.

"I require no assistance, particularly from so unwilling a savior," I informed him.

"I do not doubt it. But perhaps that victim does."

We rode for some time without speaking, ever climbing. The horrible screams came infrequently, but often enough to assure me that we were on the proper track.

Try as I might, I could not suppress a surge of empathy for Florian, now that I imagined what he must endure as Prince Chamber Pot. Certainly he had tormented me countless times, most of all in my dreams. Yet he also spoke tenderly of his mother, treated his friend Johannes with admirable kindness, and described a romantic notion of love that in a different setting, with a different man, I would have passionately endorsed. While I could not abide the prince, as a just and compassionate soul I must treat him with the same consideration I would any other . . . and defend myself from his accusations.

"I never intended such humiliation," I said.

The prince started at my interruption. "I beg your pardon?"

"That night—the attack. I had no intent of *soiling* you. I simply wanted to bop you on the head with a rock. But the spell failed me."

Florian snorted. "So it was incompetence, not malice, that guided your hand?"

"Yes!" I answered, even at the time wondering to what exactly I was admitting.

"Is it incompetence that leads you to ruin my sleep, and of late my father's as well?"

Now came my turn to frown: "What—I mean, I beg your pardon?"

"You feign ignorance? Night after night you invade my dreams—though I would far more enjoy that lovely vision than its living counterpart."

"*I* am in *your* dreams? I might beg instead that you depart mine! And you, too, are far more pleasant in dreamland than in reality—I daresay that asleep you have the makings of a true suitor!"

"Not that you would ever know," he snarled.

"Not that I would ever want to! Nor would I give one moment of my life to 'invade' your dreams. How arrogant you are! I do not need this ridiculous chatter, I do not require your aid, and I certainly do not appreciate you and your father lurking like vultures about my castle! Begone!"

At once Florian reined his horse about and shot downhill.

Furious, I dug my heels into my pony's sides. Yet again the man had captured what little composure I fancied myself to retain and destroyed it utterly. If he and his pathetic coterie deserted Montagne this very instant, 'twould not be soon enough. How dare he believe I sent myself into his dreams—

At this, I flinched. A "lovely vision"—so he had described me. Was it possible his dreams mirrored my own disturbing visions of a doting and delightful prince? That as he slept, *I* was equally attentive to *him?* Hot blood raced to my cheeks, and in furious embarrassment I drove my pony onward. O dreadful thought. I must not waste time musing so.

I had responsibilities—somewhere above me lay a man in great suffering. I was a healer. I was a *princess.* I would comport myself thusly.

❀ ❀ ❀ ❀

The chill alerted me to how far my pony had climbed. Ancienne's peak stood somewhere above, the mountain's breadth blocking it from view. We entered a hollow so deep and sheltered that last year's snow lay banked yet in its shadows. There, prone in the middle of the glade, lay the crumpled corpse of a man. I had arrived too late.

Then the wind shifted, the air swam with sulfurous gas, and without warning my pony, as horses everywhere are wont to do (the exception of course the noble steed of Saint George), reared in terror, tossing me to the ground, and fled downhill at a gallop.

I lay there, stunned by my pony's unprecedented display of ill manners, when a heavy scraping noise caught my ear, and at once all reason fled my brain.

Out of the shadows slithered a most utterly terrifying monster. The black-scaled beast was thrice the size of an ox, its batlike wings tattered with age. Filthy wisps of smoke oozed from its nostrils, and claws as long and sharp as scythes scratched the rocks. The beast burped, and a belch of flame puffed between its yellowed fangs. Bleary, lidded eyes peered in my direction, and it sniffed the air, seeking me out.

Help, a voice—a small, scared voice—whispered inside my head. *Help.*

"Help," I whispered aloud. "Help. A dragon." I should flee, I recognized vaguely, but I could not budge, for terror had turned me to stone.

Ever closer the dragon crawled, its pace quickening. It stank of sulfur and rot, and slime dripped from its eyes. It belched again and fire licked its nostrils. A scream rent the air—I recognized it belatedly as my own—and the dragon, leering, reared up—

A disturbance, some sound—I knew not what—caught its attention and it turned, sniffing the breeze. This gesture somehow released my paralysis and I scurried behind the nearest tree. The beast, noting my disappearance, released a hoarse roar of flame.

"Ben! Your pony—it bolted . . ." shouted a familiar voice, and Prince Florian burst into the glade, sword drawn. He caught sight of the dragon and stepped back. Whatever he had been anticipating, this was not it, and daunted indeed he appeared as the monster faced this new disturbance.

In truth, I was no safer negotiating the dragon's aft, for its long tail lashed like a whip, sending up hailstorms of gravel. I retreated desperately from this onslaught ere I was slashed, or worse.

The dragon swiped at Florian, and the prince leapt back in the very nick of time.

"Look out!" I cried, unnecessarily. Again the dragon struck at Florian. Bravely the prince feinted, parrying his outsized opponent as best he could.

Now safely beyond that awful tail, I realized I must offer some assistance. My dragon-fighting skills being what they were, I had no plan, but in a fit of bravado I picked up several rocks and commenced hurling them at the dragon's thick hide, praying the distraction would provide Florian a respite. The rocks, alas, soared far wide of their mark, one practically grazing Florian's head.

"*At* the dragon!" he shouted. "You're supposed to throw them *at* the dragon!"

"I'm trying!" I shrieked back.

The dragon turned toward my voice. I screamed in fear, and again brave Florian stepped into the monster's path, drawing its attention.

Retreating, I stumbled on my little healer's kit, thrown

with me from the saddle. Surely it contained something useful! Ointments, herbs, bandages, needle and thread (for what—mending? Mother carried them), a scalpel—perhaps that would work.

With an angry shout, mostly for my own benefit, I hurled myself at the dragon's flank, swinging the blade at the beast.

The scalpel bent in half against that scaly hide. Ignoring me, the dragon swung at Florian with a great roar, knocking him sideways to the ground.

"Ben! Magic! Where is your magic?" the prince cried in desperation.

"I can't!" I wailed. What good be elemental fire against a flame-breathing dragon?

The creature sent a triumphant burst of flame at Florian, who at the last second hurled himself beyond reach of this blast. We were doomed, both of us—

But wait. There was a possibility—the smallest, slimmest thread of possibility—that I might yet make some contribution.

The dragon caught Florian with a blow that split his scalp.

I ripped off my riding habit and brandished it wildly. "You

there—Hideous! Get away from him, you sniveling excuse for a beast!"

The dragon, posed over Florian, one clawed foot pinning him to the ground, peered back at me. Venom dripped from its open jaw.

"Yes, you!" I shouted. "You pathetic, worm-faced, scabrous lizard! Get over here!"

"No," gasped Florian. "Do not sacrifice yourself . . ."

"Sacrifice?" I shrieked. "The sacrifice today shall not be human!" I was more beast than human at this point and, as if to prove it, with my free hand magicked a ball of fire that I hurled between the dragon's eyes.

The gauntlet had been tossed. With a rumbling growl that shook the trees, the dragon marched toward me.

"Oh, you're quite the monster!" I sneered. "You should try eating *me!* Not him! He's all muscle and sinew. You want to eat me—nice, fleshy me, don't you?"

The dragon rumbled its eagerness, stalking me across the glade. I had no escape. If my plan did not work, I would die, but death at least would come quick. The beast was too enraged to prolong my execution.

With a flourish, I tossed my riding habit aside and planted

myself, arms outstretched, a perfect target. The dragon took one last lunge, I recoiled backward—and tripped, falling into the deep snow preserved in the shadowy gloom.

I can only imagine the horrifying spectacle that followed. The dragon plunged its fearsome snout into the bank, grasping me between its teeth. Florian screamed, but too late—the dragon tossed back its head and with one enormous gaping motion swallowed me whole.

What transpired next I did not have opportunity to witness, to my everlasting disappointment, so some portion of this description remains conjecture. The dragon turned from this scene of infamy, en route to its next victim. It burped, but the belch included a great cloud of steam. The dragon paused and peered down at its belly in puzzled concern. With an ear-splitting whistle, enormous clouds of steam erupted from its open jaws. The dragon began to gag violently as steam poured from its mouth and nose. It staggered, coughing, the steam gradually abating until only wisps seeped out. Sagging to the ground, the dragon attempted one last time to burp up fire, but the flame in its gut had been extinguished. With a deep groan, the beast dropped its head to the ground and perished.

"Ben!" I heard Florian cry. "Oh, no!"

Shivering with cold, I eased my head out of the snow bank. The dragon lay sprawled before me, its corpse awful to behold. "It worked!" I exclaimed in disbelief.

Too wounded to move, Florian could only gape. "But you're not—it ate you . . ."

"No, it didn't," I said, climbing out. "And avert your eyes, please." I was clad only in camisole and petticoats, which the melting snow had rendered quite transparent.

Noble man that he was, the prince acceded to this request, though he spluttered and gasped as I dressed.

"It was not me he consumed, but my double, turned to ice," I explained as I knelt at Florian's side, clutching my healer's pack. The man was punctured from the dragon's claws, an awful gash above his ear; perhaps a bone was broken as well. "We must get you help."

"My father—he went . . ." Blood ran freely down his scalp. I ripped the lining from my gown and pressed it to his head. This wound, I knew, could not wait.

"I'll need to stitch you up," I said, trying to control the palsy in my hands as I dug for the needle and thread.

"Do you know how?"

"No. I'm a terrible seamstress"—I daresay not the best response I could have tendered.

"How marvelous," he murmured. "I'm not going to die, you know."

"Of course you're not." But at that moment I caught sight of his doublet.

"What is it?" he asked.

"Nothing." I forced a smile. "Nothing at all." But it was. Droplets of pus-colored dragon venom bubbled on the cloth, mingling with Florian's blood. If the venom had entered his body, it would not bode well. "I'm going to start stitching now. I'll try not to hurt you."

"You couldn't hurt me." He smiled faintly. The poison had reached him, I could tell. His face was green, and his eyes rolled back in his head. "We're going to be married."

I paused in the act of threading my needle. "What?"

"We're going to be married. I know it."

"Because of the prophesy? I revived myself. You won nothing—"

Groping, Florian found my hand and squeezed it as best he could. "Nay, not the prophesy. We will marry because I love you."

I stared, and he smiled again at my amazed face. Still holding my hand, his head cradled in my lap, he let his eyes drift shut and passed to another world.

TWENTY

Alone with Florian's body, I stitched his wounds more carefully than ever I had finished a handkerchief, and washed them clean with water from my own two hands. These tasks I did not complete consciously, but with the automatic reflexes of a woman in deep shock. With time the prince looked so presentable, stretched on the alpine flowers, that it might have been possible to imagine him only dozing, were it not for the poisonous green of his cheeks.

In this way I maintained my composure until the first men, led by King Renaldo, burst into the clearing. Then I broke down completely as the king, sobbing, buried his face in Florian's chest. The soldiers turned away, granting him some small privacy, the tears that ran down their faces scarcely less effusive.

"He died to save my life," I whispered. The great hulk of the dragon, stretched behind us, told the rest of the story.

"Would that he never died," wept the king. "But if he must, he should die so nobly."

The Drachensbett soldiers did not return to Chateau de Montagne until dusk, the keen wail of their grieving preceding them, and they bore the prince on a pine bower. The king, beside them, appeared more dead than alive.

Standing at the castle gates, Sophia observed this procession, and I was stunned to see a tear working its way down her expressionless face. "We shall escort you tomorrow to your home." She paused, struggling for words, and, bowing to the king, spoke no more.

The prince was laid in state in the great entrance hall, his soldiers standing guard through the night until he would be carried to his final resting place. Unable to watch, incapable of aiding these men with their work, I fled. Alone in my chambers, I locked my door, for added precaution wedging my sturdiest chair beneath the knob, and with a furious lunge stepped through the wall.

The wizard room was as I had left it. Dust gathered on the floor, the mice marking it already with their own obscure tracery. On the lectern, the book rested, tightly closed.

In fury I slammed it, pounded it, to no avail. "How can I save him?" I roared to the room. "How can I save him if you will not give me the spell? He was poisoned—I can save him yet! Help me!"

My screams faded in the stillness. I panted in frustration, glaring at the skull-shaped locks. The mirror caught my eye, and swiftly I wiped it clear. "The prince has been poisoned," I hissed at my reflection.

"You know that already," my reflection replied.

Yet again her nonchalance took me by surprise. Now that I had her attention, as it were, I did not want it squandered. My thoughts worked at one another like a hundred quarreling blackbirds. Abandoning for the moment my efforts with Florian, I returned to my reflection, at last able to speak these words: "My father is dead."

My reflection nodded.

My father lay near the peak of Ancienne. The dragon—a dragon that men for generations unknown had spoken of—truly existed, atop that mountain . . .

I raced back to the mirror, the realization coming to me at last: "A dragon killed my father."

No reaction. Furiously I smashed my fist to the pane. Why would it not agree?

Although, I realized, if the dragon had killed my father, how did he come to perish in the cave? I tried once more. "A dragon gravely wounded my father."

"Of course," my reflection replied in her irritating manner.

Another lightning-bolt revelation: "That same dragon killed my mother and uncle."

"Yes," my reflection drawled, examining her nails.

"Which means"—I spoke to myself now, rather than the mirror—"that Drachensbett had no role in their deaths." If Drachensbett had no role—if the king was not guilty, if Florian was not . . . Oh, my feelings were in such a horrible muddle!

"I must save the prince!" I cried out.

"Why?" asked my reflection coldly.

I blinked. In the turmoil, this question had not crossed my mind. "Because he saved my life."

"You saved it yourself," said my reflection in the same cold voice.

'Twas true. I had. I paced. I was so very tired. "He should not be dead because he is a good man," I said at last.

"So, too, are many corpses," my reflection replied with a voice of ice.

I pondered. "He is clever, and witty, and chivalrous. And handsome, too."

"Why do you say such things?" my reflection prodded.

I waited. I would not be baited so. I would not grovel.

"You know the truth," she added, more softly.

"What do I know?" I pleaded, groveling at once. What did I know about the prince? "I know that . . ." My voice broke. "I know that once, in a different time, I liked him even though I should not. I know that . . . that I may love him."

"Then you know what to do," my reflection whispered. "You know how the story always ends."

"I do not!"—and, suddenly, I realized I did. With a cry of triumph, I hurled myself toward the stairs. Yet I could not resist racing back to the mirror. "It is nice to see," I told my reflection, "that you are finally making yourself useful." With that, I returned on winged feet to my chambers.

❀ ❀ ❀ ❀

I had not realized how late it was—or rather, how early. Drunk with exhaustion, streaked with cobwebs and dust, I more resembled beggar woman than princess when at last I stumbled into the great hall.

Outside the entranceway, dawn tinged the mountaintops.

Within, six strong men lifted the prince's body, now encased in a coffin of glass, to their shoulders. The king, gaunt and aged, stepped forward. Drachensbett soldiers fell into formation behind him, then courtiers, all facing the rising sun that would light their cheerless journey home.

"Wait!" I called from my vantage point on the stairs. My voice, ringing out at that moment, could not have been more jarring, and the pallbearers paused less from courtesy than shock. Sophia, monitoring this ceremony, eyed my soiled form.

"Please," I continued, hurrying down the steps, "might I see him one last time?" The desperation in my voice must have carried some weight, for with great reluctance the men lowered the coffin to the ground.

I knelt, touching the lid. "Remove this, please. I beg you." Reluctantly, glancing sidelong at King Renaldo, two soldiers did so.

Even now, Florian looked striking, however deep the wounds cut into his lifeless flesh. I touched his cheek, traced my hand along it—feeling the beard there, the beard he had teased me, so long ago, for lacking. My tears fell on his cheeks, and I studied him, his dark brows and long lashes, to remember him always, should my efforts not succeed. I had not even thought of this during the hours I had prepared his body. Perhaps if I had attempted it yesterday, I would not have succeeded, for the power of magic stems not from its application but by the truth behind it.

I brushed a lock of hair from his forehead. The moment hung in the air—if not now, never, but if I failed . . .

"Your Highness," murmured the king behind me, and I felt his desperation to depart.

I leaned forward and kissed Prince Florian as he so many times had kissed me in my dreams. I kissed the man I loved, whom I would love forever and ever with all my heart, for he was my own true love.

Embracing him, I wept for the failure I had been, for the companionship we shared and that I through my harsh words had broken. I wept because the prince in his own way had forced me to mature into a true princess yet would never know this. And my tears mingled with my own sweet kiss, and at once I felt his lips move against mine as he kissed me in return, and his arms closed around me, and the hall erupted in cheers and sobs as the men and women there witnessed their greatest hope returned to life.

And so it was that Prince Florian of Drachensbett and Princess Benevolence of Montagne were joined in holy matrimony, and my perilous adventures came at last to an end.

❀ ❀ ❀ ❀

Every fairy tale, it seems, concludes with the bland phrase "happily ever after." Yet every couple I have ever known would agree that nothing about marriage is forever happy. There are moments of bliss, to be sure, and lengthy spans of satisfied companionship. Yet these come at no small effort, and the girl who reads such fiction dreaming her troubles will end ere she departs the altar is well advised to seek at once a rational woman to set her straight.

Thus will I take this moment to describe our life together, though I need first attend to several details overlooked in the passion of my narration. As I ultimately deduced, both my parents and uncle were victims of a vicious dragon to which the Drachensbett army had no relation whatsoever. This explained as well the inexplicable sheep snatchings, the disappearance of several wandering shepherds, and the death of the dragon's last victim, a young man who had arrived in Montagne only the day before with the goal of scaling Ancienne. His death was tragic, to be sure, but perhaps not so tragic for a mountain explorer, and in later years his grave became a pilgrimage site for men of equal ambition and madness.

In due time, and to prove to King Renaldo the wisdom of the specter that had appeared at his bedside, I led an expedition to the highest reaches of Ancienne, inventing my own "dream" as justification. Renaldo accepted this fantastical explanation with the fervor of a recent convert, and if Sophia did not, she held her tongue with her usual inscrutability. Together they assembled a crew of soldiers and explorers, and Hildebert as well, for she hailed from mountain stock and insisted on participating that she might protect me from bears.

Beginning from the glade in which the dragon had perished (and which was already the material of legend), we soon intercepted the Drachensbett trail and followed it to the mountain's ridgeline. Turning toward the peak itself, after only two hours' labor we discovered the cavern. With torchlight we examined the words Walter had scratched. His final greeting—FAREWELL, SWEET BEN—had double meaning, recognizing so tenderly his daughter while acknowledging as well the heir to Montagne's throne. As for his other phrase . . . shame reddened my cheeks as I at last read it properly.

Not I PURSUED DRACHENSBETT, but I PURSUED DRAGON HERE.

Sure enough, not two hundred paces away soldiers discovered the dragon's own den, devoid of riches but full of bones and rock and the armor of Xavier the Elder. "Doubtless he gave the beast indigestion," murmured Xavier the Younger, fingering his father's helmet, and one could tell that the man's death would forever be a source of pride to their clan.

Florian for his part transported several well-preserved dragon droppings to the main hall of Fortress Drachensbett, where he displayed them in a neat glass case. His battle with the dragon had raised his standing considerably among his soldiers, and by now flaunting the source of his nickname, he silenced the mockery completely. Such is the finesse of a natural leader.

As to the dragon's actual death, I can explain it only partially. Having recalled from a childhood story the imperative of fire for dragons' existence, I deduced (in a lathering panic, lest one forget) that water might thus work as toxin to the beast. In a spasm of spell work I cannot fully construe and hope never to be forced to replicate, I at once created my own frozen Doppelschläferin, remembering in my haze the spell book's warning on frostbite. The dragon gulped down my double, and the melting ice promptly snuffed its fire and killed it dead. The creature, granted, was half dead already, and if anyone challenge my solution by claiming this, I invite him to attempt the same against any healthy young dragon of his choosing.

Perhaps the oddest event in this series of misadventures came about one afternoon as Sophia, Renaldo, Florian, and I dined al fresco with the nobility and personages who had gathered for our impending nuptials. Renaldo spent the meal so distracted that I could not but worry over the insult that Montagne must have inadvertently proffered.

He rose to speak. As conversation died, he turned to the queen and asked in a voice of heartbreaking modesty for her hand in marriage.

Had the king announced he was about to whelp wolf pups, I would not have been more shocked. Now, however, I recalled his frequent praise of Sophia; perhaps his efforts to conquer Montagne had been due less to passion for its land than for its leader, however ham-fistedly he chose to display this.

The queen's reply gave me a second shock in as many minutes: "We most gladly consent."

Once it dawned on me that the union might mean the loss

of their excellent counsel, my enthusiasm lessened to the point that I debated banning it, as was my right as head of state. My rational side prevailed, however, and the situation was resolved admirably. For several years following their marriage, the couple resided in Chateau de Montagne, pursuing their devotions. King Renaldo (forever known by this title, though Florian held the throne) laid out in Montagne's rich soil a harmonious garden, spectacular in all seasons. In the garden's very center rose a small villa, designed by Queen Sophia for them both. The laborers toiling day and night could not but admit, when the project ultimately concluded, that it was indeed the loveliest structure any of them had ever seen, and to this day it remains the "jewel of Montagne."

It is worth reiterating that the prophesies ultimately proved true, as prophesies with proper time and insight forever do. The prince did awaken me—not with a kiss, but with blunt words that opened my eyes, however painfully, to my many shortcomings. In attempting to spite him, I perversely transformed myself into a woman too worthy of rejection. Florian delighted ever after in pointing out this fact, particularly at moments when my pride threatened to overwhelm my great good sense, when he would lift my hand to his lips and, kissing it, murmur smugly, "I won."

Indeed, this became such a jest between us that on more than one occasion requiring utmost solemnity, his act of lifting my hand to initiate some formal procession would reduce me to uncontrollable giggles—shockingly indecorous but nonetheless amusing to the dignitaries and crowds observing my temporary collapse.

The second prophesy came true as well, though I am inclined to think of this less as prophesy than edict, for King Renaldo accepted the words of that dream specter far more readily than ever he had those of day-lit diplomats, and he never again attempted possession of our little kingdom. Florian was crowned King of Drachensbett and Prince Consort of Montagne, where he lived with greatest delight in Chateau de Montagne to the end of his days, though he traveled regularly to Drachensbett to attend to matters of state and the fruit harvest.

We have an expression in our country: "The proof lies in the bottom of the pot." I admit that I never ruled with the authority or passion of Queen Sophia, but now, at the bottom of my own pot, my country yet stands intact, its people as healthy and content as people ever have a right to be. And so I dedicate this work to her memory as well as that of my parents, for however we might criticize those who rear us, the fact that we survive at all into adulthood, however late that passage comes, is testament enough to their ability and perseverance.

With humble regards,

Her Royal Majesty Benevolence of Montagne,
Queen of Drachensbett, and Defender of
Ancienne and Its Many Secrets